DogDaze

Published by Barbour Publishing, Inc., P.O. Box 719, Uhrichsville, Ohio 44683, www.barbourbooks.com.

Our mission is to publish and distribute inspirational products offering exceptional value and biblical encouragement to the masses.

Printed in the United States of America.
Dickinson Press, Inc., Grand Rapids, MI 49512; February 2012; D10003168

Dog Daze

Lauraine Snelling *and*
Kathleen Damp Wright

the S.A.V.E. Squad

BARBOUR
PUBLISHING

Dedication

Lauraine:
Dedicated to basset rescue organizations everywhere

Kathleen:
Dedicated to my parents

Acknowledgments

Lauraine:
I'd like to thank Dawn at Daphneyland
Basset Rescue in Action, California, for time
and encouragement in all things basset.

Kathleen:
Thanks to *The Daily Drool* for questions answered on what
Wink might do. Thanks to Blue Water Resort in Garden
City, Utah, for the free extended stays at the condo for
writing; and Sue's and Ramona's stories to remind me why
I like to write. Becky and Louise for all the reasons they
know and don't know in the adventure of girlfriend-ness.
Thanks to my students for their "what box?" creativity and
bug-eyed thrill that I'm publishing a story.

From both of us:
Always grateful for our husbands: Lauraine's Wayne and
Kathleen's Fred for accepting that this is a viable way to
live and have adventures. Our gratitude to God for all the
dogs that have graced our lives with unconditional love,
hysterical behavior, and saliva.

God, You are our Forever Home.

Chapter 1

Countdown to Total Humiliation

Five empty seats left. Five chances remaining for total humiliation.

Don't pick me, don't pick me, don't pick me. Aneta Jasper's plea zipped through her mind. Kind of like when Grandma zipped the two of them through traffic on the electric pink scooter. On this June Friday, the Oakton City Community Center auditorium was hot and crowded with sweaty kids her own almost-sixth-grade age.

The stage gaped like a monstrous mouth, the eight chairs on its edge—like teeth. A microphone stood in front.

Aneta closed her eyes as the mayor of Oakton City's raspy voice announced the first three of eight winners of the Founders' Day poster contest. She didn't want to walk up in front of all these people. She didn't want to sit on that stage. And she didn't—*didn't*—want to speak her bad English into that microphone. She also hadn't wanted to enter the contest in the first place. Mom's idea. At the thought of her adoptive mom, Aneta smiled even while she clutched her stomach.

"Remember, these winners become Junior Event Planners for our Founders' Day charity fund-raisers," the mayor remarked, looking up from her notes. "Next winner, Melissa Dayton-Snipp."

Junior Event Planners? Fund-raisers? Aneta's eyes flew open. Her throat dried up. She swallowed, adjusting the headband that held back blond hair skimming her shoulders. The words in the application had been too hard to read. Aneta had simply signed the form and handed it in. The ache in her stomach grew. She was glad Mom had left today for a work trip. She'd be home Thursday and wouldn't see Aneta embarrass the family by losing. . .or worse, by winning and standing up in front of people—and Melissa—and speaking bad English.

Aneta watched her private-school classmate, a brown-haired girl with chunky blond highlights, walk the "Melissa Walk" to the stage. Her hips swung back and forth, her head tilted up. Like she was the princess. From Aneta's arrival at The Cunningham School, Melissa had appointed herself Aneta's interpreter and American role model.

"It will be a great opportunity for teamwork and community service," the mayor said.

Uh-oh. Opportunity was one of Mom's favorite words. *Opportunity* meant Aneta ended up doing things she didn't like and didn't do well. It was hard enough learning to be an Annette instead of Aneta, a Jasper instead of an orphan, and an American instead of Ukrainian. She wanted to make Mom smile, to be a Jasper the way The Fam were Jaspers: loud, smart, and—brave. So she'd said yes to the contest. The more she said yes, the less they might send her back.

Four chairs left.

Aneta shivered. Now more than ever, she did not want to,

could not win. Speak and then be in a group? "Don't pick me, don't pick me, don't pick me," she muttered again, hands tucked under her capris, staring down at her lime-green sandals, bright against the tan of her narrow feet. She'd rather be home in the pool.

Someone nudged her. Opening her eyes and turning toward the nudge, she looked into the curious almond-shaped brown eyes of the girl on her right. The girl's black hair was pulled back in a high ponytail that shone under the auditorium lights.

"You okay?" the girl asked. "I'm Vee." She stuck out her hand.

Aneta had yet to get used to Americans with their hand shaking. Vee was the first kid to do so. Aneta slowly offered her own hand, and Vee pumped it briskly.

"Me?" Aneta swallowed, reminded this was her answer to nearly every question. "I'm okay." She would bet Vee was the confident kind of girl who would be good at everything and probably got picked first for PE.

"Vee Nguyen," the mayor announced. She pronounced the last name as "new-winn."

The girl smiled, showing straight, white teeth. "I knew it." She leaned to whisper in Aneta's ear as she rose. "I have an awesome idea for a fund-raiser. Plus I did a makeover of the Oakton City logo. In calligraphy."

"Oh." Aneta nodded as if she knew what Vee was talking about. The theme had been "Looking Back and Looking Ahead." Her own drawing, in Prismacolor colored pencils, had been more memory than great art. The tall, stone orphanage where she'd spent the first ten years of her life had been easy to sketch, as well as shading in the outlines of stray cats and dogs that hovered around the gates waiting for fresh garbage.

Mom called it "profound." Aneta thought it just looked sad. Animals and kids nobody wanted. She'd been one of the lucky ones, adopted by Mom, a lawyer, and into The Fam, the kind-yet-strange bundle of grandparents, aunts, uncles, and cousins.

Three seats left. Aneta resumed the singsong in her head.

"Esther Martin," the mayor announced.

The dark-blond-haired girl on Aneta's left, who filled her own chair and spilled over a little against Aneta's leg, leaped to her feet. "I have a great fund-raiser all planned," she hissed to Aneta and began to push past knees to the aisle. Her yellow T-shirt with big letters: AND YOUR POINT IS? stretched tightly over her stomach. Long, dangling earrings bounced against her perspiring face.

Some of the kids whispered as Esther's rear end bumped past. Aneta felt bad for her and thought her brave. During the school year, kids had whispered and laughed about Aneta's bad English. She spent a lot of time hiding in the bathroom. She hoped they wouldn't taunt this year, now that she was in sixth grade—or would be in September. It was summer; she could ride the Pink Flamingo scooter during the day with Gram, swim with Mom in the evenings and on weekends, and not worry about her English.

Two chairs left.

"Sunny Quinlan."

A yelp of pleasure echoed through the increasingly stuffy auditorium. Across the room, a redheaded girl, shorter than Aneta—everyone her age was shorter—leaped toward the front. "Yayness!" she yelled, setting off a ripple of laughter.

That girl will have no problem speaking into the microphone, Aneta thought, lifting her hair off a sweaty neck. Sunny's smile looked like it was used to spreading across her face.

Aneta's stomach twisted sharply.

One seat.

Surely she was safe. She held her breath, preparing a relieved whoosh. She wouldn't have to pretend to faint, run out of the room, or persuade Mom to let her not be a winner.

"And finally. . . ," the mayor said, folding her paper.

Don't pick me, don't pick me.

Chapter 2

Too Many Melissas

She had been terribly wrong. She was not safe. She tripped over feet to the aisle then stumbled up and onto the stage. A million nameless faces looked at her. She looked at them.

The short, round mayor beamed at the audience. "This young girl is a new citizen of the United States. She was adopted almost a year ago." She placed a heavy hand on Aneta's shoulder. "Go ahead and tell us your name, and as a special treat, tell us what you like best about living in America."

Her name, her name. What was her name? The silence seemed longer than a day and only a breath shorter than forever. She heard Melissa whisper, "She doesn't know her own name."

"Aneta!" she blurted loudly. "I like—" What did she like about living in America? She loved The Fam. She loved Mom. She liked to eat. She loved to swim. Her mouth opened, but no words emerged. "I—I—"

She would find a phone. She would call Gram. And she would never, *never* return to the community center.

"Annette—er, Aneta?" A tall man stood in the hall, the flow of winners splitting around him. With his brown hair tied back in a ponytail, a red striped shirt over long shorts, and a tattoo covering his right forearm, he looked like a skinny pirate without a mustache. "Whoever you are. You're in this room with Vee, Sunny, and Esther." He jerked a thumb to the right.

Still dazed from the humiliation of being led off the stage by a smirking Melissa, Aneta looked up at him. Who was she? She wasn't sure.

"Where is the phone?" she whispered, gazing up at him. Be in a group? Come up with a fund-raiser? She wasn't even sure what one *was*, but it sounded quite difficult. "I call my grandmother," she finished. That English sounded wrong. Missing words? At least he would see she wouldn't fit in the group.

The impatience in his hazel eyes shifted to kindness. Melissa Dayton-Snipp swooped in the next moment, tugging Aneta through the kids in the hall to the drinking fountain.

"What a loser group you're in," Melissa said. She backed up into the final stragglers, the better to look up at Aneta. Easily five inches shorter than Aneta, she was thin and wore a summer dress. "Everyone knows Sunny's homeschooled, and those kids are always freaks. Then you're stuck with Vee Nguyen who bosses everyone. . . ."

Melissa had perfected the I'm-so-much-better-than-*that* tone in her voice.

"Throw in that fat girl Esther Whoever with the loser wardrobe. . .like she doesn't own anything other than a T-shirt?

Your group is toast." She unclenched the death grip on Aneta. Melissa excelled at gathering information—Aneta remembered from school. Melissa raised her voice to a near shout. "Do you unnn–derrrr–stand?" As though Aneta had no ears and no brain instead of slower English.

On the inside, she imagined herself yanking her arm away from Melissa and saying, "I *so* don't need your help." She would say it, too, if she thought it would come out right. She also understood, however, that girls at school who didn't pay attention to Melissa Dayton-Snipp found no other girls would pay attention to them either. Not that Aneta wanted a million friends, but she'd like one or two. She'd seen Melissa at work and didn't want to become a. . .what was the word Mom used about her law clients? *Victim.*

Aneta glanced first at the man wearing a name tag that said FRANK, who was looking impatient, then at Melissa. What to do? Run into the room and face more girls like Melissa or remain in the real Melissa's clutches?

Melissa kept right on talking as though Aneta were absorbing every word. Aneta imagined she was in the pool at home, slicing through cool water, watching the shifting blues on the bottom. The water didn't care if she spoke good English or was accepted by other kids or if her adoptive family liked her enough to keep her. Gram said it "chilled her out." Aneta hurled one last desperate glance up and down the hall for a phone somewhere, anywhere. Nothing.

Thankfully, Frank stepped forward. "Melissa, get going to your own conference room." When she hurled the Death Stare at him, he *laughed.* Aneta couldn't believe it. Then, as his gaze fell on Aneta, he tipped his head to the left. "Time to get going."

Not her. She was going for a phone to call Gram and get out of there. She stepped away from Melissa and toward the room. As she passed him, Frank patted her shoulder with a warm hand. "Don't ask me why they gave me a group of all girls, but *they*, in their infinite wisdom, did."

"Oh," Aneta said. He didn't want to be in the group either. She entered the room. Vee and Esther, who'd already exhibited so much more confidence and courage than she, sat with pads of paper. Too many Melissas. She wished Mom hadn't left on a business trip today. Wished Gram would hurry up and come get her and take her back to Gram's house.

As she took the chair next to Vee, Aneta felt the heart-dropping feeling she often experienced in school. Was she supposed to have brought something for notes? Rule Three of The Endless Rules of Melissa: Never, *never* look like you don't know what you're doing or risk "Loser." Her heart pounded and she checked her watch. Just after three. How long before Gram would come? She kept Aneta company and drove her around on the Pink Flamingo while Mom worked at her law office.

Frank's gaze scanned the girls then dropped to his clipboard. "Okay, we're missing Sunny Quinlan. I hope she gets here pronto."

At that moment, a redheaded flash wearing an oversized white tee atop khaki cargo pants dashed into the room, flip-flops flipping. Sunny Quinlan had arrived. "Hey, gang. Sorry. I got talking to a girl from my soccer team. . . ."

"About time," Vee said with an exaggerated look at her cell phone and then at Sunny.

"Atti-*toood*," Sunny replied, singing the word just loudly enough to be heard. As she dropped into a chair next to Esther, she grinned across at Aneta like they were old friends. Aneta found her mouth tugging in a half smile.

"Okay, Frank." Vee dragged her laser look from Sunny to flick an intense gaze at the others. "We're Junior Event Planners. I say we have a book sale to benefit the library."

Frank nodded. "Sounds good. What do the rest of you say?"

Vee continued, "So let's list our strengths and start working."

No kid she'd met in her nine months in America talked like Vee.

"You guys. . .er, girls. . .work together, make it happen." He glanced around the table. "Everybody clear on the project?"

Clear and *want to* were two different things. Aneta clenched her hands under the table. These girls were all Melissas. One in her life was already one too many.

"Okay, everyone say what strength they bring to the group, and I'll write it down." Vee sat up straight and held her pen expectantly as she met each girl's gaze.

A curl of panic, like icy fingers around a Slurpee, wrapped around Aneta's spine. What *strength* they brought to the group? She didn't even want to *be* in the group. She would die right here at the table.

"Hey, you're not the boss," Esther interrupted, her hands leaping to her hips in protest. "I already have an idea. We can paint the city fire hydrants like different little characters."

Sunny wrinkled her nose. "Let's come up with a rock-socko *fun* project."

Esther ignored Sunny, her eyes fastened on Vee. "You're not

the boss," she repeated, her tone not even a *bit* friendly.

"Okay, girls," Frank said.

"We need organization," Vee answered Esther in an equally cold tone. "My teachers all say I'm an organizer."

That was the testy start to twenty minutes—Aneta timed it on her waterproof watch with the stopwatch—of Vee and Esther arguing. They both wanted to be the boss of everyone else. Aneta remained quiet.

"It could happen," Vee said about a book sale to benefit the library, housed in another wing of the community center. "Easy."

"Not necessarily." Esther rolled her eyes. "That is *so* much work."

"For pizza sake, this is supposed to be *fun*," Sunny said, spinning around in the chair. "I love chairs on wheels, don't you?"

"Ladies," Frank said, louder this time.

Before I die, I'm going to throw up.

Chapter 3

Mystery Woman by the Lake

Aneta crossed her arms over her stomach. As much as Aneta loved Mom, this stomachache, this *day*, was Mom's fault. Another of the never-ending "cultural experiences" her adoptive mother thought would help her. Aneta tried to think of the word Mom used all the time. . . *.assimee. . .assimilate*.

Sunny turned to Aneta. "Do you speak?"

"Who, me?" Aneta's voice trembled. Maybe there would be an earthquake. Did they have earthquakes in Oregon?

A tap sounded on the door. Frank yelled, "Come in, if you dare!" He looked around the table. "You're supposed to be working *together*. It's not a contest."

Vee's right eyebrow shot up. Aneta wondered how she did that. She tried making hers do that and succeeded only in drawing Sunny's amused glance.

"*Everything* is a contest," Vee said firmly.

"Not necessarily," Esther said.

"This is supposed to be fun, girls," Sunny said.

Frank shook his head.

A short, stocky boy with redder hair than Sunny's stuck his head in the room. "The mayor sent me to get your idea. Melissa already told her group what they're doing." His laugh—a high, croaky cackle—bounced around the room. He grinned when he saw Aneta. "Hey, Annette the—"

"Aneta," she blurted. What was wrong with her today? Almost a year ago, before they drove to court to make her adoption official, Mom had asked her again if she liked the name Annette. She'd said yes. It didn't seem to matter then that she would no longer be who she had been. But today, when C.P.—who was her neighbor across the back fence—had called her by her American name, "Aneta" had slipped out. Maybe that's why she'd said her Ukrainian name with the right pronunciation—Ah-NETT-uh. It wouldn't rhyme with the nickname "Annette the Wet" that C.P. found so screamingly funny.

"We don't have a fund-raiser yet," Sunny said, standing on her tiptoes and stretching her arms over her head. "And we are *not* having fun." She glared at Frank.

"It's not *my* fault," Esther said. Her bottom lip shoved into a pout. "Hi, C.P.," Esther said then pounced on Aneta as C.P. said, "Whatever," and slammed the door behind him. "So do we call you Aneta or Annette?"

Aneta wondered how Esther knew him then forgot him as the group quieted. These girls were waiting for her to tell them her real name. This was her chance to act like a Jasper, be bold and brave. Nobody had called her Aneta since she had left the orphanage with the child aide worker. While it wasn't uncommon for adopted kids to change their names with their new life, Aneta had yet to feel like an Annette on the inside. Moistening her lips, she said quietly, "Aneta. . .yes, Aneta."

Aneta sighed. Now that C.P. knew, Aneta would have to try to explain the name issue to Mom. Not only had Mom given him permission to join The Fam "Pool Plashes," so he would be underfoot, but C.P. lived to broadcast what he knew.

"Let's refocus, please," Vee reminded the group. She used a lot of Mom words.

"It's not like you're in charge," Esther shot back. "If you weren't so bossy, we'd have our own idea by now."

"If you'd skip the drama—" Vee's pen carved a hole in the paper. She snapped her lips together.

Sunny started laughing. Aneta wanted to crawl under the table.

Staggering to his feet like he carried a heavy load, Frank made a time-out sign. "That's it. You guys are outta here," he said, jerking his thumb toward the door.

Relief flooded through Aneta while the other three protested. It was finally over. She was halfway to the door when Frank's voice stopped her.

"Hold on, Aneta." His voice turned stern. "I want the four of you to take a break—down to the lake and back—and figure out how to solve this teamwork issue." He raised his eyes toward the ceiling. "I get three drama queens and one nontalker." He shook his head. "The things I do to pay the bills."

The first one through the door toward freedom, Aneta could have told Frank she'd already figured out the answer. A group of *three* Melissa types—as in *not* including her—would come up with a great Founders' Day fund-raiser.

Even though the late-afternoon sun popped sweat on Aneta's forehead and made her squint, the ever-present pine scent helped lower her shoulders from her ears. So did being out of that room. She picked up her pace to a near jog, anticipating the peaceful blue of Trail Lake. She and Aunt Jardine often rode their bikes on the path around it.

Once the girls met up with her, she would say she was quitting. She made a face. The Fam were not quitters. They talked about that a lot. But this was a special reason. It wasn't quitting if you couldn't do something, was it?

She was nearly to a run by the time she glimpsed the lake through the trees. She could hear the *thud, thud* of the three behind her, with a breathless Sunny shouting pleas for Vee and Esther to stop blaming each other that the group wasn't "cohesive"—Esther's word, whatever it meant.

"Aneta! Wait up!"

Aneta slowed but didn't stop.

Sunny ran in front of her and began to spin in a slow circle. "I give up," she said breathlessly, arms out as she spun. "Those two are on some control trip, and I don't have a ticket." She staggered to a halt, her smile wobbling. "This is not really your thing, is it?"

Aneta met Sunny's eyes, started to shake her head, and then stared over Sunny's shoulder. A woman, barely noticeable through the trees, was walking toward the shore. A white garbage bag hung from her arm.

Sunny turned toward the lake. "What are you looking at?

Hey, who is that? She looks like my little brother does when he's sneaking around."

"That bag. . .it is moving. Something sticks out—" Barely had the words left Aneta's lips when Sunny grabbed her arm and yanked her behind the nearest pine tree, so big Aneta could not have put her arms around it.

"Don't let her see us!" Sunny hissed.

Moments later the other two joined them.

"What are you doing?" Esther's voice sounded impatient.

"Shh!" Sunny's freckled face looked like she'd just found a million dollars. "We're doing a Nancy Drew, stalking a potential criminal. See the bag? It's got holes, and there's something sticking out." Pressing her face against the tree then drawing away with a disgusted sound, she picked at her face. "Eww. Pine pitch."

A snort from Vee. "Nancy Drew is *so* fourth grade." But she kept her voice low and peered through the branches.

The woman began to swing the bag.

"Okay," Aneta whispered suddenly, feeling Vee was being unfair to Sunny. "I like Nancy Drew."

The other three girls drew back, looking at Aneta like she'd just said she had a purple head.

"You talk?" Vee and Esther spoke at the same time, looked at each other, and laughed.

Well, even if she wasn't going to remain part of the group, at least she'd made them smile. She grinned back. Sunny, who had turned back to watch the woman, smothered a shriek. "Something long and skinny is sticking out! Gotta be snakes!"

"Could be toxic waste." That was Esther.

"I sure wouldn't want to be swimming there after she throws

it in," Sunny said.

Aneta shuddered. She wasn't afraid of snakes on the ground, but the idea of one touching her in the water. . .

The woman stood back a bit from the water's edge and whirled the bag like a slingshot. On the second revolution, she let it fly.

"Good-bye, snakes," Esther murmured.

As the bag hung suspended, a very unsnakelike sound split the shimmering heat. The woman sprinted away from the shoreline and disappeared down a side trail. For a breathless second, the girls froze, then:

"It yelped!"

"It can't be!"

"She's murdering a *dog*!"

"Run, run!"

Pelting down to the shoreline, Aneta watched the white garbage bag hit the water, eliciting another series of horrifying howls and yelps before it sank beneath the surface.

Chapter 4

Help! Murder! *Frank!*

At the sound of the girls' screams, the woman jerked, turned toward them, and then shielded her face with her arm and took off at a dead run toward the line of trees. At the same time as the four of them left the paved road and pounded down the gravel boat-launch ramp, she had nearly reached the stand of evergreens that closely circled the lake.

Esther and Aneta stared at each other, unbelieving. Sunny took off running. "She—she—" spluttered the redheaded girl, changing direction toward the retreating woman. "Hey, you! Stop!" Her curly hair floated out from the sides of her face like wisps of cloud. Before Aneta's brain told her, "*Go!*", Aneta's body had jerked into action. The long legs, so accustomed to churning up pool water with the endless laps, sprinted toward the water's edge and the wooden dock. She kept her eyes on the ever-widening circles of tiny waves. She pumped her arms forward, putting more force on the toes of her Teva sandals. *Go, go, go.*

"Save it! Save it!" shrieked Esther from behind.

Behind her, Aneta heard Vee holler she was going for help.

Her swim instructor, who worked as a lifeguard, told her you never take your eyes off where you saw the person go down. Only the last bit of white garbage bag broke the ripples surrounding it. At the end of the dock, she slowed long enough to grab each sandal and fling it from her then braced herself to push off the end of the dock. She knew from picnics with Gram at the lake that it dropped off quickly into deeper water. Once the bag sank beneath. . .

"Ow!" Her right foot slipped on an uneven board. Her arms flailed to regain an upright position. In she tumbled. Lake filled her nose and eyes. As she blinked to see underwater, she heard a dull *clunk*.

She could only think, *I took my eyes off the victim.* She fought to regain the surface and not think about the puppy struggling to breathe. How long had it been since they'd seen the woman's arm arc forward, sending the bag and its contents into the lake?

The ripples were wide now. Was there any hope? Her arms sliced the water while her legs propelled her forward. Right toward the middle of the ripples.

How far out was she now? She didn't know. Then she saw it, the blob of white just under the surface. She gasped, choked on some water, and switched to the breaststroke. Every second counted.

Ignoring the bursting in her lungs and the burning in her legs, she kicked once more and barreled toward the bag, right arm outstretched, left arm pushing through the water like a steering wheel. She grabbed the bag.

Treading frantically, she raised the bag out of the water. A chubby arm reached in front of her and yanked the bag away. Shaking water from her eyes, she found the rough wooden side of the rowboat inches from her face. Limply, she reached up to hang on. A pair of hands wrapped themselves around her arm and began to pull.

"I've got the dog. Are you all right?" It was Esther's high, nasal voice.

Still gulping air, Aneta let Esther pull her until it began to hurt. "Ow!"

"I'm trying to pull you into the boat."

"Help—dog." She gasped, trying to catch her breath. "I float." She wrenched her arm from Esther's and floated onto her back toward shore, letting each muscle unclench as one of her cousins had taught her.

It had been The Fam's first July Fourth picnic after she'd been adopted. "Breathe in, breathe out, and relax," he'd said. That day the sky had been a bright blue and not a cloud to be seen. Aneta had been bursting with happiness with her new life. Today the sun skipped in and out, and its glare smacked her eyes painfully. Still, she knew where the shore was and headed there with strong sculling, feeling the swish of her shirt and the flare of her capris against her skin. Had she made it in time for the dog? At the memory of the high-pitched yelps, she gasped and inhaled a nose of cold water, which made her choke—again. Then her thoughts turned to Gram and the soaking clothes. Would she be angry that Aneta got her clothes wet? For a second, she tensed and began to thrash in the water. She could hear voices behind her on the shore, hear the banging of oars and Esther with the puppy headed for shore. Her throat clogged.

The puppy would not have a chance.

She knew that. She'd had that thought even while swimming with all her might. Even with Esther rowing hard, there would not be time to save him. Would anyone even know how to save him? How much could girls do? The orphanage supervisor was fond of saying as much. *"There is only so much one person can do about anything, Aneta."*

When her heels hit the mud, Aneta rolled to her side and stood up awkwardly, wiping the tears from her eyes. She'd done her best. What if it wasn't good enough?

Chapter 5

Soggy Puppy

Esther met her as she walked out of the lake, wringing water out of her hair.

"You were amazing, Aneta." Esther pulled her toward the group kneeling in a small circle. "They've got the puppy over here," she continued, keeping a strong grip on Aneta's arm. "I was praying my guts out that you wouldn't drown *and* you'd save the puppy."

"Is—he—" Aneta's breathing sounded hoarse to her ears. She felt like she'd swallowed most of the lake. She coughed, clearing her throat. If Esther's prayer had come true. . .

"Frank's wife, Nadine, is working on him now."

Aneta followed Esther's chunky frame the few steps to the group. Leaping up from her crouched position near the still doggy form on the mud, Sunny threw her freckled arms around Aneta and began to cry. "You were incredible," she said through her sobs. "When I was trying to catch the murderer, Esther was already dragging the boat into the water. That girl is strong! Vee sprinted—I mean, the girl can run—then Frank came." She was gasping too much now to continue talking, and she bent over, hands on her knees.

Aneta glanced at Frank kneeling in wet shorts next to a woman with long hair so black it glowed blue in a sudden burst of sun. She held the puppy close to her face. The long, straight bangs hung over the black, brown, and white puppy and his long, drooping ears. His eyes were closed.

A sour smell, too familiar from the orphanage, wafted to Aneta's sensitive nose. She looked down at the dog. Sure enough, a thick puddle of tan and green foamy ick lay on the woman's knees. Suddenly Aneta gasped, shuddering.

Sunny clutched her arm. "Is she—?"

"Yes," Aneta said, slapping a hand over her own lips.

The woman had her mouth over the dog's wet, chunk-covered snout. With short, quick puffs, she blew into the loose-skinned mouth. *How can any air get into that long snout?* wondered Aneta. How long had the puppy been without air?

A deep trembling began in the bottom of her stomach. She wrapped her arms around her middle, suddenly feeling cold. That feeling was familiar and not a feeling she wanted to feel. It meant she might cry. When she cried, she very often couldn't stop. She sounded ugly when she cried like that.

"Somebody—call—somebody." Gulping, she threw a desperate glance at the redhead. Sunny shook her head, momentarily taking her gaze from Nadine working on the puppy. "This is a dead zone for cell phones. Just here, on the boat-launch area. That's why Vee took off running. Her cell had no bars." She patted her shorts pockets. "And I am not privileged to have a cell phone until I'm thirteen."

A snuffling snort punctuated the murmur of voices. The

puppy's sides heaved violently. Nadine backed up just in time for another spew of yellow foam that cascaded over the young woman's knees. In the interim, Aneta had somehow landed on her knees in front of the puppy. Droopy lids lifted to reveal saggy, mournful brown eyes. *Well,* Aneta amended, *one brown eye.* The right eye was a strange milky blue and squinted, so the pup looked like he was winking at her. He blinked.

"Wink," she said softly. "You are Wink."

They were almost at the community center side door when someone finally spoke.

"How could someone do that to an animal?" Sunny bounced along, her red, fluffy hair glinting in the late-afternoon sun. Her fierce expression shone with sweat. She looked like she was ready to punch the woman wearing the beige Crocs and cap. Aneta had no doubts that she could land a few good ones. "I wish I'd caught her. If I'd had a cell phone, I'd have taken her picture and gotten her on *America's Most Wanted.*"

Will Wink live? Aneta wanted to shout the question and interrupt Frank, but her voice wasn't working once again.

He was answering Sunny. "Some people, when, for whatever reason, the dog doesn't work out, treat it like trash and simply throw it away. They don't think animals are valuable, that they are living things that need to be cared for." Frank's stride was long, and the girls scrambled to keep up.

"His eyes are weird." Esther's voice was matter-of-fact. "He wasn't perfect."

Sunny spun around, hands on hips. "So what? Nobody's

perfect. That's no reason to *drown* him."

The other girl regarded Sunny and shrugged. "I'm just saying maybe that's why the woman threw him out."

"Esther has a point. Some people don't want a dog that isn't perfect. But really. . ." Frank moved into a trot. The girls followed. "We need to find that woman. What she did is against the law. Besides being flat-out wrong."

"Wink will live?" It was Aneta's voice. Finally. She pulled her wet tee away from her. It felt chilly, even in the heat. Gram would be sure to ask about *that*!

Everyone halted and eyed her. Frank was the first to speak. "Wink?" he asked. "I thought you girls said you didn't know the woman."

That familiar *uh-oh* stomach clutch struck with that many pairs of eyes on her; Aneta regretted spitting out the name. He had become Wink to her when he opened his eyes after Nadine breathed into him. He'd looked right at her, and he had been frowning, the extra skin above his eyes folding deeply. And then he had winked. At her. Saying thanks.

Vee appeared from around the side of the community center. "Nadine called and said the puppy is at the vet. They are going to at least keep him overnight to see. . . Well, to see." She shrugged.

"The puppy," Esther said. "Aneta named him Wink."

A slow smile, the first one Aneta had seen, curved the wide mouth. "Hey, you're right. The puppy does. He's got one eye that's pretty squished. When he blinks—"

"He winks!" Sunny and Esther chorused. "Aneta, you're brilliant. That *has* to be his name!"

"Anyway," Frank said, walking in the door. The girls lengthened their strides to follow him. "Wink's lungs sounded like they needed help."

"Is he going to die?" Aneta asked. She swallowed hard in a dry throat. If her best hadn't been good enough. . . She wished Mom weren't on a trip or that Gram were there. She searched the parking lot for her grandmother's Pink Flamingo scooter, but it had yet to swing into the half-circle parking lot. Mom wouldn't be home until Thursday. Aneta bit her wobbly lower lip.

Frank surveyed the four sad faces in front of him. He sighed. "Oh boy. This wasn't in the job description." Leaning against the door, he folded his arms and stared at his sandals. "I'm not going to lie to you girls. This is not a perfect world."

Vee waved her hands in front of her, signaling frustration. "We're eleven years old. We've seen stuff. Is he or isn't he?"

For a moment Aneta heard a buzzing in her head, and Frank's face swirled in front of her. The wish that had begun when Wink winked at her pushed further into her bones. Aneta thought her heart might shatter if Frank said what she thought he was going to say. Now that she had a family who said they loved her and had a home, she had hoped her heart might stop breaking. Now her stupid heart was cracking again. Over a soggy bunch of wrinkles who probably wouldn't live. Wink.

Chapter 6

Mission: Make Mom Love Wink

On Wednesday, Gram remembered. They'd spent the day shopping and taking a walking tour of the historical district in a nearby town. A great day, but Aneta was tired. She had her head tipped back, eyes half-closed, watching the trees and the sunlight speckle over her head. The trip had been planned to help Aneta with being sad over the short life of Wink, but it hadn't worked. He was all she could think about. Gram abruptly pulled to the side of the road.

"On Friday, when you ran inside your house to change out of your wet clothes and grab your duffle bag, what did you do with the lake-stink-and-vomit clothes?" she asked, removing her helmet and turning to her granddaughter.

"Um. . . ," Aneta said, removing her own helmet.

"That's what I thought. So they've been where? On the floor of your room since Friday?"

"Oh no," Aneta reassured her grandmother, knowing that the hardwood floors did not do well with wet clothes. "I put them on the washing machine."

"*On* the washing machine, not *in* the washing machine."

"Yes."

Gram jammed the helmet back on her head. "Put your helmet on—we need to make a detour to your house."

Half an hour later, rather than heading straight to Gram's, her grandmother pulled the Pink Flamingo through the security gate, down the lane, and turned right into Aneta's driveway. "You grab the clothes. We'll wash them at home. I'll check the answering machine."

Aneta hit the fridge for a bottle of water on her way to the mudroom and the clothes. The ride had been warm. Once in the fridge, she pulled out a couple of leftovers she'd been supposed to take to Gram's on Friday. Making a face, she dumped them in the trash, containers and all. Good thing she'd remembered to at least throw them out!

"Aneta!" Gram called from the living room. She appeared in the kitchen with the scooter keys jingling in her hand. "Accelerate, granddaughter. What meeting is a Frank talking about at the children's section of the library in"—she glanced at her watch, also waterproof with a stopwatch like Aneta's—"*five minutes*! Time to rock and roll!"

Nine minutes later, Gram dropped Aneta off at the doorway of the library. Gram told her to call her when the meeting was over. "Then you can tell me what this is all about. Does your mother know?"

"Um," Aneta said.

"I thought as much. Call me when you're done." The helmet went on and Gram drove away.

As Aneta approached the children's section with its red, yellow, and blue flags fluttering from the rushing air-conditioning ducts, she heard Esther's high, nasal voice.

"We need a plan we *all* agree on, not just you bossing us."

She ducked behind the stacks that blocked the girls from seeing her. She did not want to be part of this group. She'd been hoping since Friday that Frank would forget about her and go with the other three girls. They certainly did not need her. She closed her eyes and remained motionless. *Think calm, cool, pool water.*

"Well hi, Aneta!" Sunny's bright voice sounded near her. Her eyes flew open as Sunny twirled past. "Good thing you're here. I hope you have good ideas. We are not getting along." She pulled Aneta around the stacks and toward an empty, large desk. The nameplate said NADINE, CHILDREN'S LIBRARIAN. Aneta could hear Vee and Esther quarreling but could only see the tops of their heads. Why were they sitting on the floor?

Suddenly the two girls giggled. "Oh, squish alert. He's so stinking cute!" That was Esther's voice, almost a coo.

Then she heard a puppyish, "Aroo! Arooo!"

Her heart squeezed. *Could it be?*

Sunny grinned at her. "Cool, huh! We were all surprised when we showed up."

In three steps Aneta was around Nadine's desk, legs trembling. There stood a small wire pen with blankets, a water dish, and an overturned food dish with a couple of bits of food around it. There, also, was Wink. He lolled outside the pen between Vee and Esther, ripples of puppy wrinkles squishing up around his face as the girls petted and rubbed his belly. Every now and then he grunted like a piglet, as if saying, "Don't stop!"

"He is alive!" Aneta cried, dropping to her knees.

Nadine returned to her desk. She smiled at Aneta. "We just

weren't sure he was going to pull through, and when you girls didn't call us, we decided we better wait before telling you how he was. We almost lost him two days ago, and then he seemed to perk right up. He's a survivor, that dog. Then Frank said you hadn't come up with your idea yet—"

"Our fund-raiser!" Vee said, scooting her legs back and jumping to her feet. "We have to agree on something." She pulled out her phone and checked the time. "I've got to leave in ten minutes."

"Where do you have to go?" Sunny asked. She had dropped to the floor and was on her stomach, her face nose to nose with Wink's. A long pink tongue—not Sunny's—flicked out and licked the redhead's face. She giggled, scooped up the puppy, rolled to a sitting position, and cuddled him. She glanced up, noticed Aneta's face, and shoved the puppy toward her. "Here. You named him."

Soft, warm. *Alive.*

Vee ignored Sunny's question after spearing the girl with a glare. "What's wrong with a book sale to benefit the library? I love the library."

Aneta, holding the puppy under her chin and giggling as the quick licker washed her neck, said without thinking, "It is more important to find the Crocs Killer."

The three girls swung around toward her. Aneta flushed. Had that been her voice sounding so. . .bossy?

"You actually can talk when you want to, can't you?" Sunny's warm smile took any sting out of the words. "You're right. We'll find her and bring her to justice." Sunny pulled her usually smiling face into a fierce frown. "She'll be sorry she messed with us."

Now that Aneta had spoken, she was at a loss. How would

they find a woman of whom she had only caught a glimpse and noticed she wore the same kind of shoes Gram did? Those plastic Crocs Gram had in rainbow colors. In the intervening moments between the shock of hearing the puppy yelp, Aneta had noticed only a hat and the beige Crocs. Not much to go on.

"Finding her might be a bit hard since we didn't see her face." Vee set down her notebook, pulled the ponytail holder from her hair, and plunged her fingers through it. Then she drew in a sharp breath, checked her phone again, and yanked her navy backpack onto her back. "I've got to go. We are going to get in trouble if we don't come up with a plan." She glared at the group and took off at a run through the library toward the glass doors.

"Guess this meeting's over," Sunny said, smiling like it didn't bother her. "Frank is not going to like this."

"He is definitely in a learning mode with you girls. He's coached basketball and taught kayaking and river running, but you four. . ." Nadine shook her head. "I'm sure you'll all figure out a plan in the end."

Plan? Aneta now had a plan. The plan had jumped from her heart into her head the second she'd seen Wink rolling on the carpet. Bring Wink home. Forever.

Aneta called her grandmother, and then the three remaining girls walked outside and spied Vee just disappearing off to the right.

Esther squinted. "I wonder where she's going. She sure didn't want to say where."

"I will adopt Wink," Aneta said suddenly then covered her mouth with her hands.

At that moment, a pink scooter zipped into the turnaround at the front of the community center.

"A scooter!" cried Sunny and Esther in unison. And then, looking at each other, they laughed together for the first time.

"I love scooters," Esther said. "They're so cute."

"Eco-friendly, too." Sunny's eyes glowed. "Look, the driver is taking off her helmet." In another moment: "It's a grandma lady!"

Indeed, the woman who stood up, still astride the bright pink, shiny scooter, had short gray hair that curled over her head. Or rather, as Aneta knew, that *would* have curled over her head if the helmet hadn't squashed the curls into helmet hair. Her grandmother ran from her house, five miles away, to Aneta and Mom's house and back regularly. She could beat Aneta in the pool easily. And that was just the beginning of her activities. Days with Gram meant Aneta fell into bed at night, nearly asleep before she pulled up the sheet.

Now the woman was moving toward them.

"When I get my driver's license, I'm going to have a scooter." Esther talked more to herself than anyone else. "That way only the person *I* invite can be with me."

"Annette, darling!" Gram's familiar greeting. She picked up her pace. Aneta was pretty sure no one in the world could walk faster than Gram.

Two heads swiveled toward Aneta.

"That's your grandmother?" Sunny turned, open mouthed, toward Aneta. "She rides a pink scooter? How cool is that?"

"So, what is it? Annette or Aneta?" Esther folded her arms across her T-shirt, which showed a brilliant sun and dancing children above the words This Is the Day the Lord Has Made and bored her gaze into Aneta. "You never said."

Because I do not know.

She stepped forward, hugged her grandmother, and gestured toward the girls who were watching her expectantly.

"And the meeting was for?" Gram prompted with a grin.

"These are the other girls who won the poster contest for Oakton Founders' Day. Vee had to leave."

"Yeah," Esther said quickly, "and she didn't want to tell us where she went."

Sunny jumped in. "We won Friday, but finding Wink kind of stopped our brainstorming."

Gram shot Sunny a quick look before applauding the girls. "Congratulations, winners! I didn't know"—another glance at Aneta—"the awards were Friday. The Fam would have been there for sure. I know your mother would have liked to come."

Her face might as well burst into flame and be done with it. Belonging to The Fam meant every occasion was a group occasion, complete with loud cheering. They would always attract attention. You'd think by now she would be used to it. Maybe even say her opinions loudly, like The Fam. Laugh a lot, like The Fam. Get in trouble with their mouths, like her cousins. But she didn't. She liked staying out of trouble. It was easier that way. If she didn't get in trouble, well, they wouldn't send her back.

Gram stuck out her hand toward Sunny. The redhead took it and then squeaked. Aneta winced. Gram had a crusher grip.

"I'm Sunny."

Gram shook Esther's hand. "You're the winners then?"

"Wow," Esther said. "You make us sound important. And we don't even have a proj–"

"We don't have a fund-raiser yet!" Sunny shrieked, clapping her hands to her head. "You guys!"

Out of the corner of her eye, Aneta had seen Esther glance between her and her grandmother when her grandmother called her "Annette." Time to get out of there before any *more* questions. Like about her adopting Wink. That had slipped out.

"Hi, Gram! I am ready." She turned to the others. "Good-bye."

"Wait—Aneta—" Esther placed a hand on Aneta's arm. "We have to meet to get a plan. Melissa already has hers. And for finding. . .you know who." She gripped Aneta's arm. "What's your phone number? We need to set up a time to get our project!"

"Aneta?" Gram's brows shot up. Aneta didn't dare look at her. Gram turned expectantly to Aneta.

"Uh. . .uh. . ." It was happening too fast. When Gram nudged her, however, Aneta quickly spilled out her address.

"What about meeting tomorrow at Aneta's? After Aneta's mother gets home, after dinner? I'll call her." Gram patted her pocket.

Aneta wanted to get out of this group, not have it come to her house. If these girls came tomorrow, they would get in the way of Mission with Mom that was growing brighter and brighter every time she thought of Wink.

"The Gates?" Esther asked, eyebrows shooting upward. "Vee told me her mom lives right around the corner from there." Jamming her fists into her pockets, she added. "We're on Aspen Grove."

"Aspen Grove? That's the street where my brother's piano teacher lives. It's like a block away from our house," Sunny said.

"Is Mrs. Nissen your brother's piano teacher?" Esther asked, hands on hips. "My brother walks to his lesson every week. Where do you live?"

Sunny's eyebrows shot up. Then she began to laugh. "We all

live within a block of each other."

"And we've never met," Esther added. "Vee bragged she was gifted and talented at Oakton Elementary." She pointed to herself. "I go to Oakton Victory Academy, same Christian school as C.P., that boy from the community center. Anyone else a Christian?"

"I am," Sunny said with a smile. "My parents are home-schooling us. We call our school Quinlan Christian Academy."

Aneta remained silent. Gram nudged her.

"I go to The Cunningham School," she said softly then added, "where Melissa goes."

"Oh, you poor girl!" Esther cried, rolling her eyes.

Aneta couldn't wait to put on her helmet and swing her leg over the scooter to get away. Any plan to get out of the group was not going to work now that Gram knew about it. In addition, Aneta would have to come up with a second plan—the plan to convince Mom that Wink needed a home with them.

Chapter 7

A Not-So-Great Start

The next day, Aneta sat by the pool, deep in thought. Mom was coming home today, so she had to have a plan for Mission: Make Mom Love Wink.

"You've got a problem," said a voice across the patio. Aneta looked up to see C.P. hanging over the six-foot fence. He was so short. How did he do that? One of these days, she was going to go into his yard and find out.

"How do you know?" she asked. Sometimes C.P. said puzzling things. Life as Aneta Jasper—Annette?—had suddenly gotten very complicated. She desperately wanted a few turns in the pool to relax. But Rule for the Pool: No pool when there isn't an adult. Plus her plan had to be finished before Mom came home from work. A quick glance at her watch showed she had about an hour from the time Mom's plane landed and she arrived home.

"You want Wink to have a forever home with you."

"Yes." She leaped up from the chair and ran through the patio door and up the stairs two at a time. In her bedroom, the oak desk stood by the large bay window overlooking the pool. Aneta took a deep breath, telling herself that if she continued to shake, she wouldn't be able to hold the pencil. That would not help Wink come home. She yanked open the middle drawer on the right. Once armed with a medium-sized sketch pad and current favorite pencil, she pounded down the stairs again and sat down at the patio table. C.P. still hung over the fence.

Now. To steady her hands. And draw. She took in a deep breath. The pool lay next to her, blue and with just the tiniest ripples from the fake clown fish moving through the water. She smiled. C.P. had given it to Mom after she said if The Fam was over, he could join them in the pool. That kid loved their pool.

"A forever home," she said, rolling the words around in her mouth. They sounded safe.

"My mom calls God that," the boy said matter-of-factly, as though he were sitting next to her instead of hanging over a fence. "Someone who never goes away."

A forever home. Yes.

"That is what I want," she said. Back to the mission: Bring Wink Home. Step One: Artwork. How to start? When Aneta had drawn the poster, every line and shading reminded Aneta of her previous life. The pencil had seemed to move on its own. Now she wanted the pencil to do the same. *Think.* Why had a soaking-wet little basset puppy captured her heart?

Her pencil lay still in her hand, acting as though it had never encountered a sketch pad. Wink was an orphan, like her. Little droopy Wink. The sag of the good eye and the squint of the bad eye. How he really did wink. The pencil began to scratch, slowly at first as she retraced each moment of the afternoon—from the first sight of the woman flinging the bag into the water, to how her lungs had nearly burst reaching for Wink as the bag sank, to

Wink's weak hurl on Nadine. Her pencil began to speed across the paper.

She'd completed his eyes and had just begun the broader strokes of both his ears when she heard Mom's familiar greeting through the intercom connected to the front gate of The Gates.

"Honey, I'm home!" Mom said it every night.

Aneta jerked her head toward her watch. Early! With a desperate glance at the half-finished portrait, Aneta leaped to her feet, dropping the pad and pencil. One step toward the door then two leaps back toward the patio chair. Stay and finish? No, she always greeted Mom at the door to the mudroom. She scooped up the paper. She had to do everything right tonight. If she could show Mom how responsible she was, tell her about winning the contest—that Mom made her enter—and then show her Wink's portrait, surely Mom would see Wink needed to come home.

At the threshold of the patio door, she stopped short. Oh. There was the Aneta/Annette thing. The telephone rang, but thinking about this was more important. Maybe the Annette/Aneta thing would be tomorrow night's project. Suddenly so many projects. This was summer vacation!

"We must adopt Wink. He is an orphan like me. He is so cute. You will love him." She began to practice what to say to Mom as she skipped toward the garage door. Every workday she would meet Mom in the mudroom by the garage. Mom's blond hair might be falling out of the low ponytail and her blue eyes might be tired, but they would brighten when she saw Aneta.

"My girl!" she would say, extending her arms for a hug. The Fam was big on hugging. Aneta found she liked it very much. After a quick stop at the fridge for sparkling water for Mom and Mom's special lemonade for Aneta, the two of them would walk arm in arm out to the pool in nice weather. This is where Aneta would complete the simple Step Two: Wink's story. Step Three would be easy: Mom says yes.

As Aneta rounded the corner of the mudroom, however, she saw Mom standing by the washer and the open door to the garage. Standing with a pile of wrinkled clothes in her hand, a frown creasing her forehead. Aneta could smell the clothes from where she stood. Lake stink. Dog vomit. Six days of sitting. Her gaze traveled up to Mom's face. Most of Mom's hair had escaped her ponytail. Her eyes were more tired than Aneta had ever seen when she looked up from the clothes in her hand.

Uh-oh.

"I—I—" began Aneta. Suddenly she didn't know where to start. The long list of what had transpired since Friday tied her tongue. The paper in her hand crinkled and she looked down at it. Wink. Yes, Wink. "You are home early."

"Yes, my conference finished early, and I ran for an earlier plane." She raised the pile of clothes to her nose then made a face and held them away. "Why are these clothes on the washer? And why"—she stopped and sniffed—"do they smell like the lake"—another gingerly sniff at the wrinkled, stinky mess—"and vomit?" Alarm flashed in her eyes. "Are you sick, sweetie?"

"I—I—" Why hadn't Aneta remembered the yucky clothes the day she took them off? Or when she and Gram came to the house yesterday? Mom looked so tired; she needed some good news. Aneta glanced again at the drawing in her hand and raised it to Mom's eye level, drawing in a deep breath. "The Crocs Killer threw Wink in the lake. We saved him. He needs a forever home—" She stopped short. If Aneta had learned one thing about Mom, it was that "just the facts" worked better than a wandering explanation. "I—I—I won the contest. I made new friends." That second statement was a bit of a stretch. She didn't think she could call Sunny, Esther, and Vee *friends* exactly.

"You won the contest!" In an instant, Mom's frown had cleared; her eyes brightened. She clutched the clothes to her chest. "Congratulations, sweetie. I knew your poster would touch people." She gestured to the paper in her daughter's hand. "But what is this? That's not the orphanage drawing."

Aneta removed the clothes from Mom's grip, set them back on the washer, and drew her by the arm toward the kitchen and the fridge. Time for sparkling water and lemonade. *Note to self: from now on, watch out for the stupid laundry.* Mom worked hard. Aneta could do her part. This next conversation must go perfectly. While she took two tall turquoise plastic tumblers from the cupboard and filled one with lemonade and the other from a bottle of sparkling water, Aneta plunged in. "I would like to adopt Wink, a basset hound someone tried to murder the other day. He is an orphan, like me."

The telephone rang, but they both ignored it.

Mom remained motionless, leaning against the island counter. Not even a twitch of her eyebrows. Her gaze had traveled up from the sweating glass Aneta had set in front of her to Aneta's face. Long moments ticked past. At least it seemed that way to Aneta. She must have said too much too fast. Would she have another chance?

"You would love him," she said, feeling desperate. Step One had been easy, even though it had been interrupted. Step Two wasn't working. She hadn't even gotten to how she had rescued Wink, how he'd winked at her, and how he wasn't dead and needed a forever home.

"But, Annette, you're not an orphan. You're a Jasper." Mom looked puzzled and, well, like Aneta had punched her.

Annette. One of the other projects. *For pizza sake*, as Sunny would say.

"Um, Mom, about—about my name." Now what should she say? She inspected her smudgy hands holding the sketch.

Mom's face furrowed into worry lines so deep her entire face seemed scrunched. Had that not been the right thing to say either? This was hard. How to get back to talking about Wink?

The front doorbell chimed. Aneta's mother hunched her shoulders, stretched her neck, and sighed. "If that's my family, I'm telling them no Pool Plash tonight." She stood slowly, as though she were pulling up through cement. Passing by Aneta, she squeezed her daughter's shoulder. "It seems we need to talk."

Chapter 8

A Waddle Is a Winner

So she *had* gotten through! Good. Oh. Another flash of inspiration hit. The Fam. Wait. Sketch in hand, she followed Mom through the family room toward the front door. Telling The Fam to go away was not good. *I need them.* Of all nights, she needed them there—to argue, to yell, to laugh, and to help Mom know they needed to give Wink a forever home. To convince her to take Wink away from being scared and put him in a place where everywhere he turned, he kept running into a hug and a smile. Maybe one of them would even suggest *first* that Mom and Aneta be his forever home.

Mom opened the door. Aneta peeked over her shoulder. How many cousins had come with Gram tonight? The group of three on the front steps, who were *not* The Fam, waved at her.

Uh-oh. Aneta had completely forgotten both the project *and* the group of Melissas.

"Oh hi, Aneta." Esther's louder-than-necessary voice. The girl waved at her.

Mom looked at Aneta. Aneta looked at the girls.

"Nobody answered the phone, so I thought I would just walk around and pick everyone up. We all live so close! I hope you don't mind." Esther's eyes were now surveying the roomy family room with its fireplace that could be seen on both sides—both from the kitchen and the family room. Comfortable burgundy leather love seats and oversized footstools filled the room, with colored-glass lamp shades over wrought-iron lamps on the table. "We're late turning in a fund-raiser idea for Oakton Founders' Days."

"And you're so cool to let Aneta adopt Wink!" Sunny stepped forward, her voice bubbling like Mom's sparkling water. "Can you believe that Crocs Killer tried to drown him?"

Oh, if only The Fam had descended instead. Aneta considered saying she was suddenly sick and running up to her room. No good. She was rarely sick. She eyed the phone on the long coffee table. Only a few steps away. A quick call to Gram. . . She began moving toward it.

"Crocs Killer? Aneta?" Mom repeated.

Oh dear, this was getting worse. Aneta took her hand off the phone, thinking fast.

"Hi!" she said, her voice sounding as loud as Esther's. "Mom, these are my new friends from the community center. Now we are a team!" She searched Mom's face for signs that she was shifting away from the shock toward the new *good* news.

It worked. Mom smiled. She shook her head the tiniest bit. "Oh, Annette! Teamwork is great." She stepped forward and wrapped her arms around Aneta, her head only slightly taller than Aneta's. "I knew it was a good opportunity."

Vee spoke. "There's a problem, though. We don't have a fund-raiser to present to the city council yet." She jerked her chin toward Esther, her eyes slitted. "Some of us are not team players."

"Yet," Sunny said quickly, stepping forward with a smile. "Can we hang out for a while and come up with our project, Mrs. Jasper?"

"*Ms.* Jasper is great. And it's great you girls are working together." She backed toward the kitchen, waving toward the patio. "Go ahead to the patio and start brainstorming. I'll bring the lemonade and thaw out some cookies."

Aneta cast a longing look at the phone as she led the girls through the door and onto the cool stone patio. Esther, next to her, hissed in her ear, "Thaw out cookies?"

"Yes, my mom makes peanut-butter cookies when she is— well, a lot. Then she freezes them." It had been a tough month for Mom. She'd lost two cases. Jaspers didn't like to lose. The freezer was full of cookies. Mom called it her "therapy."

Esther closed her eyes and smiled. "I love peanut-butter cookies."

After the girls had dropped into chairs around the glass-topped table, Vee pulled out her notebook. Aneta shot a glance toward Esther. The girl was already frowning. Any time Vee whipped out the notebook, Esther's face settled into grumpiness. Aneta sighed. Maybe it would have been easier to be in the real Melissa's group. At least then there would only have been one of her.

"So, how come your mother calls you Annette, but when C.P. called you Annette, you said Aneta. What's the story?" Sunny was consuming peanut-butter cookies rapidly, filling one hand as soon as it was empty and holding one in reserve. Vee daintily nibbled around the edges of her first, while Esther eyed the plate, hands folded in her lap.

"By the way, these cookies are killer."

Pride rushed through Aneta. Even Gram said nobody could make a peanut-butter cookie like Mom.

"Yeah, and how come you always say 'Mom' instead of 'my mom' or 'my mother'?" Esther's right hand snaked along the table until it encountered the cookie plate. She snatched one off the plate and stuffed it in her mouth. Aneta remembered girls at the orphanage doing that with bread at dinner and felt sad. "Like she's just *a* mom and not *your* mom."

"I—I do not know."

Sunny brushed a couple of crumbs off the front of her shirt. "I say it's none of our business. Just tell us what you want us to call you." She looked expectant.

"I want you to call me Aneta." It was out. Again.

Half an hour later, they were no closer to agreeing on an idea. Sunny had deserted her chair soon after polishing off her lemonade and several cookies and was pacing around the pool, snapping her fingers as she thought out loud. Vee and Esther interrupted each other on every idea.

Aneta said nothing. She was thinking plenty, however, as she continued to draw Wink's ears then move down his baggy throat. She did not care about Oakton Founders' Day and the fund-raiser. She only cared about bringing Wink home and finding the Crocs Killer. While the voices swirled around her, she continued to plan. First, after the girls left, she and Mom would have their talk. That would take care of Wink's forever home. Then she and Mom could "brainstorm," as Mom liked to say, about how to bring the Crocs Killer to justice.

The clink of ice brought her back to the patio action. Mom had stepped through the french doors with the turquoise pitcher. "More lemonade? How are the cookies holding out? What ideas are you getting for your fund-raiser?"

Esther smiled at Mom. "The cookies are great. So's the lemonade." She straightened in her chair and glared over at Vee, who was draining the last of the lemonade from her icy glass. "Some of us can't agree on anything." Vee narrowed her eyes over the rim of the glass. The Vee Stare, Aneta had named it. Sunny groaned loudly. Aneta thought of Wink.

As Mom set down the pitcher and filled the plate from the plastic container, she glanced at Aneta's sketch. "Oh, sweetie, you've gotten so much further on that. It's—beautiful, yet so"— she hesitated, looking for the right word—"pathetic. That poor little puppy."

Sunny, who had made a beeline for the cookie plate, leaned over Aneta's shoulder. "You're good," she said, chewing. She looked at Aneta's mother. "And so are these cookies." In another second, the last bite of cookie was in her mouth and she was dusting off her hands. Her hands stilled. She dropped into the chair to the left of Aneta. Grabbing the sketch, she held it high above her head. "Guys! We have our fund-raiser!"

What was she talking about? Aneta watched Sunny prance around with the sketch.

While Mom stood holding the pitcher and smiling at Sunny's enthusiasm, the other two stopped their most recent quarrel over whether the library or the senior center should be the focus of the fund-raiser.

"What?" Esther asked.

"Explain," Vee said, her pen poised over the notebook. "I've got to be home in fifteen minutes."

"Paws 'N' Claws Animal Buddies!" Sunny danced around the table, turning the sketch this way and that. "Wink will be the poster dog for our event!"

Her little Wink, a star? Aneta's lips began to wobble into a smile. He was very cute. She would get him a new collar. *Red,* she thought.

"And what's the event?" Vee was not convinced. Her head tipped to the side. She looked down her nose at Sunny.

This stopped Sunny. "Oh," she said. "Event?"

This time it was Esther who leaped from her seat as though someone had pinched her hard. "A Basset Waddle!" she shouted. Mom started; the lemonade sloshed in the pitcher. *Esther would never need a microphone,* Aneta thought.

Aneta looked at the other faces. They showed the same lack of understanding that she knew must be on her face. She hadn't seen Wink walk yet, but with that long body and short legs, he would definitely waddle. But an event?

Seeing her audience was lost, Esther launched into an explanation. "My aunt lives in Michigan. We visited her in May. She took us to the Basset Waddle. A bunch of bassets walk in the street to a park, and everyone comes to watch them." She flopped back into her chair and began to laugh. "It was amazing! Some people dressed up their dogs in costumes. . . ." She clapped her hands. "We will be the fund-raiser for Paws 'N' Claws Animal Buddies of Oakton. The one Nadine and Frank work with!"

"We could have a costume contest!" That was Sunny. She was up and pacing the pool again. "Dogs and their owners! They pay to enter the Waddle dressed up!"

"They had a King and Queen of the Waddle—a boy and girl dog."

Aneta watched as the three girls began throwing out ideas. Vee wrote furiously, glancing at her watch now and then. Finally, after several minutes and Mom had disappeared into the house, Vee held up her hand.

"I've got to call my stepmom and ask her if I can stay a little longer." She pulled the phone from another pocket, rose, and walked away from the group to a corner of the patio.

"I wish I had a cell phone," Esther said.

"Me, too," said Sunny.

"Vee told me both sets of her parents call it the ATP." Aneta felt she should join in the conversation. After all, her Wink was going to be the poster puppy. Everyone would know he was hers!

Two sets of inquiring eyes.

"The Anti-Trouble Phone," Aneta said.

In a moment Vee was back, a frown on her face. "Okay, I've gotten an extension of twenty minutes. Then I *have* to be home or I'm in trouble."

Aneta was glad she had never been in trouble with Mom. She worked really hard at that. Oh. Except for today with the stinky clothes.

Standing straight, Vee read from her list.

"We have a Basset Waddle, a King and Queen of the Waddle—we will need to get crowns—" She scribbled a note. "Costume contest."

In a few more minutes, assignments were given to each girl. Vee laid the list on the table. Aneta saw the note about Esther and made a face. That might start another argument.

- *Crowns for the King and Queen—Sunny (How will we make the crowns stay on dog heads?)*
- *Contest entry forms—Esther (Check to make sure she spells everything right.)*
- *Pooper-scooper and bags—Esther (If her dad can get the church youth group to do it.)*
- *Stuffed basset hound toys for the King and Queen of the Waddle—Vee (My dad knows a guy who sells all kinds of dog toys.)*
- *Dog treats for dogs who are in the Waddle—Aneta (Make sure her grandmother helps her remember.)*
- *Wink's sketch as a poster with bunches of copies to put around town—Aneta (Maybe her grandmother will let us ride her scooter?)*

It did. Sunny stopped it with a shout of "GIRLS! Do I have to pull this car over?" which made everyone laugh. By then it was time for Vee to go. Vee promised to e-mail everyone a copy of the list. E-mail addresses of parents were exchanged, with the exception of Vee who had her own, and the meeting was over.

After the girls left, Aneta headed toward the kitchen. The sooner she and Mom agreed that Wink had a forever home with them, the sooner they could begin to think of ways to catch the Crocs Killer.

"We have a plan!" Aneta said, stepping into the kitchen, expecting to find Mom in the window seat with her knees up like a kid, laptop braced on the tippy top. Her hair would be yanked up in a ponytail like Aneta's, and she'd be wearing shorts and a T-shirt.

But Mom wasn't in the window seat. She was on her tiptoes in the tall pantry, her head and shoulders into the deepness of it. The top shelf.

The top shelf held the peanut-butter jar. Uh-oh. More cookies. Mom was stressing out.

"Need help?" she managed.

"No, I've got it," her mother said, avoiding her gaze for a moment. She turned away and then swung back toward her daughter. "No, I don't have it. I don't get it." Clutching the organic peanut-butter jar to her chest, she stared at her daughter desperately. "Do you not like your name? You said you liked Annette! Why do you still think you're an orphan?"

Then Mom burst into tears.

Never would she have wanted to hurt Mom. Never, as long as she lived. Rushing to Mom and hugging her and the peanut-butter jar, Aneta stammered, "I—I—"

For a few moments, neither of them said anything until Mom said faintly, "The peanut-butter jar is cutting into my rib cage, sweetie."

A bubble of laughter popped up through Aneta. She let it out, and Mom laughed a gulp laugh. Mom motioned toward the family room. They walked to the couch and sat side by side.

"Can you help me understand why you think you're an orphan, sweetie?" Mom was still holding the peanut-butter jar like a baby, close to her chest.

Aneta was silent. Why had she seen herself like Wink?

"I do not know," she said, being very careful with her English so Mom would understand. "He does not have a home. I have a home. He looked lost yesterday. I feel—" Surprise tears pricked her eyes, hot and streaming. "I am not like a Jasper. I do not argue or win." She studied her fingers in her lap. Would Mom send her back for being ungrateful? "I—I *am* grateful."

Mom sucked in a deep breath and squeezed Aneta's knee. "I see. I know you're grateful, Annette—I. . ." Here she stopped. "Is that why you told the girls you were Aneta instead of Annette?" She paused, looking up at the ceiling. "Like you feel like Aneta and not an Annette?"

She understood. Mom understood. The hard knot in Aneta's stomach untied, and she sagged against Mom. "Yes."

Mom nodded. After a few moments, when Aneta was sure Mom was going to tell her she should call herself Annette, Mom spoke. "Sweetie, if you would rather be Aneta, then I want you to be Aneta. I'll tell The Fam. If you decide in a little bit that is what you want forever, I will make the change in your name legally." She leaned into her daughter, and her voice turned stern. "But, young lady—"

Aneta cut her eyes to her mother.

"You will *always* be a Jasper. No questions about that."

"Even if I don't argue and get in trouble and speak up?"

Mom's rich, deep laugh flowed over the two of them. She stood, placing the peanut-butter jar on the coffee table. She faced Aneta.

"Even if you never get in trouble. I've actually been wondering if you ever *will* get in trouble. You're so careful, I worry. We all make mistakes. It will not change you being a Jasper." Picking up the peanut-butter jar, she waved it at Aneta. "See? I'm no longer a basket case. I'm putting the jar back on the top shelf, *Aneta.*"

Chapter 9

Oh No! Another Microphone!

$\mathcal{A}$neta craned her neck around the headrest in Mom's hybrid Lexus. Her mother caught her eye and winked. Aneta grinned. Nobody had ever arrived at an Oakton council meeting like she and the girls had just arrived.

Strung out behind Mom's car was Gram on the Pink Flamingo with a grinning Esther behind. Cousin Zeff drove his black scooter with Vee sitting straight up, her rare smile blazing. On Uncle Luke's red scooter, Sunny was shrieking something into his hairy ear. Uncle Luke was laughing.

"I know." Mom's voice held the little chuckle Aneta loved. It sounded like a ripple of water down a deep brook, like she'd been to with The Fam last summer. "Nobody attends an event like The Fam."

They parked the Lexus and the scooters side by side, with the Lexus looking like a big black mother hen next to her Easter-colored chicks. Once inside, the group gathered outside the chamber doors.

"Are we ready?" Uncle Luke had his helmet under his left

arm. With his right hand, he shoved his hand through bristly short, steel-gray hair. "Aneta, you'll do great. We'll all be in the gallery."

Aneta, who had been clutching the original sketch of Wink, jerked her head up toward him. "Who, me? I am not talking. They are talking." Those three would be good at talking. With Melissa here tonight, their group needed to be at their best. The girl could cause Paws 'N' Claws Animal Buddies some serious trouble. She didn't know how. She just knew Melissa. With another look at Wink and his sad puppy eyes she'd caught so well with her pencil, Aneta looked at Vee.

"Be sure to tell them—" she began.

The three girls looked surprised. Vee raised her right eyebrow. How *did* she do that?

"Tell them what?" Esther said. "*You're* presenting our idea." Esther grabbed Aneta's elbow on the left. Sunny claimed her right side, and they propelled her toward the double doors of the council chambers.

"Oh no. Not me." The vivid recent memory of her freezing onstage and Melissa sniggering made her stomach start to twirl around like the teacups ride at Disneyland.

"You saved us with the Basset Waddle. You tell them," Vee's voice hissed behind her, and then they were banging through the council chamber doors.

A voice came from within. "We will get started in just a couple of minutes if everyone will find their seats."

The large, dark-paneled room resembled the courtroom in which Aneta had been adopted. For a moment, she couldn't move. The memory of that day washed over her like a shower. All The Fam, a judge who smiled a lot. People asking her if she understood what was happening. Nodding her head, clutching Mom's hand.

A microphone screamed. "Ouch, Justin. You'd think by now you'd learn how to turn on that silly thing." Jerked back to the council chambers, Aneta saw a trim woman in a dark-blue suit clap her hands over her ears. She was sitting with the other council members at the raised curved table with a podium in front of it. A laptop lay open in front of her. The man at the podium rolled his eyes. Aneta smothered a grin. That lady must be grumpy a lot. He was a short man with half-glasses and a yellow, collared, knit shirt. He had a kind face. Maybe she wouldn't have to say anything. They had already given a piece of paper telling what they wanted to do. Vee and Esther called it a *proposal*.

"If everyone will take their seat, we'll get the meeting started." The council president leaned into the microphone. It shrieked again. Aneta jumped, her heart revving up higher than it ever had racing Mom in the pool. What on earth would she say?

She glanced toward the man. One side of his mouth twitched upward. He caught Aneta's stare and winked. Even in the midst of her panic, she had to smile back. She was pretty sure now that the shrieking mic was on purpose to annoy Miss Blue Suit. The woman's voice sounded sort of familiar.

She tried to relax, forced herself to lean back, and smoothed the pencil drawing of Wink. She'd finished it the day after the girls had agreed on their project. Monday, Mom went in late to work and took the four girls to a copy place to create the poster with Wink's picture on it. Tuesday and Wednesday, the Scooter Patrol, consisting of Gram, Uncle Luke who was retired and bored, and Cousin Zeff who worked it around his courier route, went to every business in town. So Aneta could join in with her new friends, Aunt Jardine drove in from Jackson in her minivan with the shelf behind it that toted her scooter. They had laughed, eaten hamburgers and ice cream, and Vee and Esther hardly even argued.

"Tonight let's move the Oakton Founders' Day business to the front so the kids can leave after they present—" The man peered over his glasses at the gallery. The Fam waved wildly to Aneta. Her cheeks burned. "Please state the community program you're supporting and then give a brief overview of your fund-raising plan."

Overview. Fund-raising plan. What did that have to do with making Mom fall in love with Wink? The whole point of the poster was to have Mom see Wink wherever she went. Then she remembered the meeting yesterday by the pool where Vee and Esther argued over proposal bullet points and lists. Sunny had kept reminding her to pay attention. *That* was why they wanted her to pay attention? She was supposed to *lead* the group?

"You can do it." Sunny gripped Aneta's arm and smiled her big smile.

Sunny was wrong. Aneta knew she would never be able to stand up at that podium and speak. Her English would fail her, just like it had at the poster awards. She glanced down. Her hands were already trembling so much the drawing of Wink rattled. She just might throw up. Really.

"Go ahead, please." His smile was nice.

Her knees locked her into her chair, rooted between Esther and Vee. Of the three, she wished the encouraging Sunny were sitting next to her. *I can't move.*

Miss Blue Suit spoke, her discordant voice with the nasal twang blasting across the council chambers. "If you are not prepared, we will move on to the next person on the list, who I happen to *know* is prepared."

"Did you girls have your project to tell us about?" The man's voice boomed over the mic, and it squealed again. A boy in Aneta's class had squeaked a balloon at a classroom birthday party at the end of the school year. It sounded like that, only so loud it hurt her ears.

She glanced over at the gallery where The Fam whispered to each other. Mom gave her the thumbs-up, a smile, and a nod. If Aneta could not get herself out of this chair, she would shame the entire family. And they had driven the string of scooters to cheer on the girls' idea of Dog Daze during the Oakton Founders' Days park festival. If she didn't get out of her chair and make the council see that they had a good idea, Wink would not be the poster dog, and Mom would not learn to love him. And what would happen after that is her heart would smash in a million tiny pieces.

She stood. Well, almost stood. She fell back into the seat.

Two rows back, a voice sailed across the silence that was getting heavier and heavier.

"I'm prepared as a Junior Event Planner, Mr. President."

Turning her head, although she already knew that voice, Aneta saw Melissa leap from her chair, a briefcase in one hand. It was nearly as big as Mom's.

"Oh, please." That was Sunny, and a snort of laughter followed the mutter. "Like she needs a briefcase?"

Making her way to the front, Melissa stood at the podium like she went there every day and loved it. *She probably does,* thought Aneta.

Her father walked with her to the podium and then drew a square box out of the briefcase. Melissa removed a laptop from the other side of the briefcase and set it on the podium. A murmur began among the watchers.

"Oh, please." This time it was Vee. "She's got a PowerPoint presentation complete with projector?" She glanced at the list in Aneta's sweating right hand and the drawing of Wink in her left. Her face descended into a frown. *She knows I cannot do this.*

"Mr. Council President, my group will support the food bank by conducting a food drive at the park during the Oakton Founders' Days. My father will, of course, provide a matching donation from Snipp's Super Saver grocery store."

The president tipped his head and peered around Melissa. "Where is your group, Melissa?"

Melissa didn't reply. With a remote she pulled from the briefcase, she clicked through a colorful, well-organized slide presentation with pie charts they had learned about in math last year. Each slide prominently displayed the Snipp's Super Saver logo.

"Excellent," Ms. Blue Suit said with a sidelong look at the four girls. "Wonderful job."

Melissa dipped her head in acknowledgment. "Thanks, Mom."

The four girls' heads swiveled between Melissa and her mother. Sunny muttered under her breath. Vee's frown hadn't lifted. Esther chewed the inside of her bottom lip.

"It looks like a crummy commercial for Snipp's Super Saver groceries." Sunny frowned and turned to Aneta. "You better un-freeze your legs and wow them with your drawing, or we're toast as Junior Event Planners!"

Melissa tossed a triumphant look at the four girls. "I will now take questions."

The president spoke. "Thank you, that won't be necessary, Melissa. We see how thorough you are. But where is the rest of your group? What role will they play in the project?"

"Oh, I'll find something for them to do that they can't mess up. If a leader is strong enough, she can make any group work." Another sideways glance at the four girls. "Whereas with a bad leader—or worse, no leader—nothing gets done." With that, her father darted forward, and the two of them repacked the briefcase. Melissa sat across the aisle from the girls. To Aneta, her look said, "See if you can top that" as clearly as Aneta knew Gram drove a pink scooter.

At that moment, a high, wispy howl rolled through the chambers.

Aneta jerked toward the back, where the double doors had opened. Frank and Nadine walked in, both holding leashes. As they neared the front, a happy swell surged through Aneta. *Wink!* She jumped to her feet the same moment the other three did.

The little puppy with the squinty eye trotted up to the front row, bumping into the larger, older basset with a white muzzle. The big basset nosed Wink back into the aisle. Frank and Nadine glanced over at the girls and stepped into the row behind them. Aneta couldn't take her eyes off Wink. The black patch of fur on his back, now dry and shining, looked like a saddle. The long, droopy ears, tripping him as he investigated the carpet with his nose to the ground, were a rich caramel brown, the color split by a white blaze down the middle.

"Are we too late?" Frank hissed over Melissa's mother's insistence that they go through the list and return to the "unprepared group" at the end.

Stepping around the edge of her row, Aneta sank to her knees next to Wink. She tipped his puppy head up and fell in love all over again. The velvety ears slipped through her fingers. Mom! Mom could see Wink. Over her shoulder, she saw Mom's head turned toward Uncle Luke. She hadn't seen him!

"Girls." It was the council president.

Aneta kissed the top of Wink's head and stood. She would do this. She would do this for Wink. She rose from the floor, walked to the chair, picked up the drawing and the list, and walked to the podium.

"M—my name is Aneta." She raised the drawing of Wink up toward the faces on the curving high stand. This was good. She had opened her mouth. "This is our—" Our what? She glanced down at the list. What was she supposed to say next? Vee's neatly typed bullet points swam in front of her eyes. Oh no. At least she'd been right about one thing. This was not like the poster awards. This was worse. Her head began to swim and not in a good way.

"We are the group who will support the Oakton Paws 'N' Claws Animal Buddies." It was Esther's voice, loud as ever.

Aneta felt the others brush against her. Sunny snatched the poster from her and shoved a warm, wriggling Wink into her arms.

"We will have a Dog Waddle fund-raiser for the Paws 'N' Claws Animal Buddies who help dogs. Anyone can come from anywhere and parade a basset hound in a costume during the Oakton Founders' Days parade. They participate for a donation and fill a pledge sheet for how many turns around the Waddle course. We'll have a King and Queen of the Waddle." It was

Vee's quiet voice. How did she do that? Aneta was still shaking, and she'd *stopped* speaking! "Paws 'N' Claws Animal Buddies does a great job. We want to help."

"And here's our reason for the Basset Waddle!" Sunny said. She dug an elbow into Aneta's side. "Hold him up!" she hissed.

Aneta's hands, full of puppy, shot into the air, as though fired from a gun. He obliged his audience with a wobbly howl. The chamber erupted into laughter.

"Thank you, girls. You have a real team effort going on there. We look forward to the Waddle." The president smiled.

"Thank you, God," Esther said softly, letting out a big breath.

Sunny turned to her. "You were praying, too?"

Aneta knew she would have if she'd thought of it. Her head cleared on the way back to their seats. The Melissa girls who couldn't agree on anything had saved the day. Wink had saved the day. She had failed, but they'd won anyway. She drew in a deep breath and turned toward The Fam in the gallery. They were standing, clapping. Cousin Zeff had his fingers to his mouth, poised for his ear-splitting whistle of approval. Mom was looking at Wink, who was now happily howling and wriggling in Nadine's arms. *Uh-oh.* Mom's face wore that peanut-butter cookie look.

Chapter 10

Big Plans, Big Trouble

So, let's make this"—Esther was standing with her hands on her hips again, but this time she was smiling and gesturing to the right—"the judges' stand."

She pointed toward one side of the park lined with tall oak trees, some of them grown from the beginning days of Oakton. Running parallel to the trees ran Park Street and five houses. Since today was the beginning of the July Fourth weekend, picnickers and families having reunions in each of the three pavilions made the park lively with running children, Frisbees, and lawn chairs next to colossal coolers.

Aneta, walking Wink in a matching red harness and leash—a present from her and Gram—was sort of paying attention. She was lost in a haze of happiness. Wink stomped along, often on his ears, at the end of a leash in *her* hand. According to Vee's plan, and Esther's grumpy agreement, the girls had met at the library to head over to the park. Fortunately, none of their families were going out of town for the holiday weekend.

There they would figure out "which way to Waddle," as

Sunny said. Vee informed them she would be twenty minutes late. Esther asked why, and Vee froze her out with the slit-eyed glare, the Vee Stare. At the library, little Wink slept in a small wire enclosure behind Nadine's desk as a children's librarian. He awoke, however, at the sound of the girls' laughing voices. The little basset tripped over his ears hustling his short legs to get to Aneta and offer his belly for love rubs.

"Squishy alert!" Aneta said, gently squeezing his loose wrinkles. Wink sighed gustily. Gram and some of The Fam would pick them up later to take them home. Via the ice cream store, if Aneta knew her Fam. The time spent waiting for Vee sped by.

After Nadine heard the girls were going to the park, she encouraged them take Wink with them. Sunny took the proffered leash. "With my brother's allergies, this is the closest I'm ever going to get to owning a dog."

Vee, whose eyes looked red, said she didn't care if she held the leash; she just wanted to get their list done. What had happened to Vee before she came? Wink made it clear, however, that Aneta was the one he preferred. As Esther took the leash for her turn, the puppy hop-stomped over to Aneta and sat on her foot, tipping his long nose and squinting up at her. Sunny and Vee insisted Aneta walk a couple of steps ahead so the puppy would bumble forward.

"And we're off!" Sunny cried. The party surged across the street and into the park.

"We'll have them waddle around within the park so they go past all the other booths and everyone can see them," Esther said.

"Fine with me," Vee said, checking off her list. "Judges' stand done."

Aneta, meanwhile, watched the little puppy's nose skimming

the ground as though he were a pirate intent on buried treasure. Squatting to stroke his smooth head, Aneta listened to Vee read off from her notebook. So far she'd come up with no memories of that day she rescued Wink. How could she find the Crocs Killer if she couldn't remember anything? The Mission Mom plan was struggling. Mom had ignored all the cute Wink stories as opportunities to suggest adopting Wink. Why, if she drove past Wink posters to work and back every day, could she say they weren't ready for a dog? The smell of peanut-butter cookies lulled Aneta to sleep several times a week.

They were doing great on Vee's list. Volunteers from Esther's youth group at church would be pooper-scoopers dressed in crazy costumes. Three enthusiastic judges were signed up who promised they did not own a basset hound. Vee's stepmom had made the fancy crowns for the King and Queen of the Waddle with little loops to go over the long ears so they would stay on. The girls' squeals over them had made Vee smile.

Gram and Aneta found a dog biscuit recipe with healthy ingredients and made many, many bone-shaped biscuits. She thought that might be why Wink loved to sniff her hands.

When Aneta told them what she and Mom had found as an additional surprise for the Waddle, the girls clapped their hands together in a high-five salute.

"We have the best group!" Sunny said.

Aneta agreed.

Suddenly the hand sniffer at the end of the red leash lifted his head. Aneta tried to pull him back toward the community center. These pastel-colored houses had been along the park nearly as long as the trees, from what Frank had told them. The poster puppy, however, insisted on snuffling his way toward the curb, leash stretched tight. For a small dog with a squinty eye, he was strong.

"What do we know about the Crocs Killer?" She gave in and walked after him, interrupting Esther telling Vee her father knew someone who had a flatbed truck they could use for a judges' stand. Vee nodded and made a note.

"What?" Vee asked, finally looking up from her list. The four girls were midway across the park. Ahead of them stood the pink-and-white The Sweet Stuff ice cream store, the Park Street houses on the left.

"What do we know about the Crocs Killer?" Aneta repeated then giggled, watching Wink. Wink had his own beat to walk by. Step, stomp-on-the-ear. Step, step, stomp-on-the-other-ear.

"We don't remember anything. It was too scary." Esther shivered.

"Let's stay focused on the Waddle, please," Vee said, but her smile was nice.

Okay, thought Aneta. I *will think harder about the Crocs Killer.* "C.P. told me a good idea for Wink's costume for the Waddle." Aneta changed the subject obediently. "He says Mom will laugh. She will want Wink because he looks cute."

"Look how determined he is." Sunny skipped forward and back. "He smells something over near that house, for sure."

"I bet Nadine is getting lots of people who've seen the poster of your sketch of Wink the Squint-Eyed Wonder Dog." Esther's voice shot into Aneta's happiness like an icy stream from C.P.'s water pistol.

Lots of people wanting Wink? She hadn't thought of that when she agreed her sketch would be the artwork of the Oakton Founders' Day Basset Waddle. The posters were in every store window and at the community center. Was she giving him away before he was even hers? What if he found a forever home other than with her and Mom? She brushed away tears as she followed Wink past the oak trees and across Park Street.

"I did not think of that." Aneta's gaze rested on Wink, straining with all his puppy power toward the last house on the right on Park Street.

Wink halted. He raised his head and sniffed. In the five weeks since the little dog had entered her world, Aneta had come to know that this lifting of the head came right before a powerful puppy lunge toward some unseen target. Her fingers tightened on the leash. Where was he going?

The girls began to laugh.

"He's got a scent!" Sunny cried, clapping her hands then looking serious. "Maybe he's caught the scent of the Crocs Killer."

A puppy and four girls trotted across the street toward a pale-green bungalow in need of paint. The front lawn was green, however, and had been mowed recently. No car stood in front of the detached garage with an equipment box alongside it. Wink pulled Aneta toward that garage of 5 Park Street, past a mailbox marked LEONARD.

"He's after something. A rabbit? A skunk? Eww, I hope not a skunk." Esther dropped back.

They were past the back corner of the house near the garage when a van pulled into the driveway behind them.

Sunny heard the muffler and turned. "You guys, what are we doing?" Sunny stopped short, her face paling under the freckles.

"What are you kids doing on my property?" The man stood half in, half out of his white work van.

Aneta froze, her arm outstretched. Wink pulled harder. A

high-pitched tone sounded in her ears. What was that? Oh, why had they come onto this man's property? Would he call the police? Would the police arrest her? That would be trouble. Mom would send her back. She tried reeling in Wink.

The man stepped all the way out, slammed the door, and regarded them from across the front of the van.

"We—" Aneta's voice failed her. Wink strained toward the garage. She had to bend down and scoop him up. He wriggled in resistance, emitting his trademark, "Aroo! Aroo!"

"Hey, get that dog away from there!" Loud.

"You girls get out of here!" Louder.

"Where'd you get that dog?" Yelling.

"I'm gonna call the cops!"

The girls turned and ran. Vee leaped over a large bag of puppy chow lying against the back door of the house. She streaked toward the community center with Sunny, Esther, and Aneta, still clutching Wink, streaming raggedly behind her.

Chapter 11

Melissa Causes Trouble

Oh, for pizza sake!" Sunny's favorite phrase jolted the three girls. She stamped DISCARD on another library book and dumped it in a canvas bin. "Aneta, we've been sentenced to this library back room for two weeks, not counting weekends, and you haven't said a word. What's up?"

Aneta stamped a book about hummingbirds and dumped it into the bin. She took a deep breath, squared her shoulders, and faced the girls.

"I get in trouble." Indeed she had. On Friday, the day of the Big Trouble, she had blurted out where she'd been and Mr. Leonard's threats to call the police as soon as Mom had come through the mudroom. It had startled Mom for sure, even taken her a few moments to reply. For a moment Aneta thought Mom was glad. Then Mom's face settled into serious. The two had discussed thoroughly that private property was private. Aneta barely slept that night, expecting at any moment to be hauled from her bed and sent back to Ukraine. By the next morning, the police had not come. The man did not call. But Mom did call the other parents; they had all agreed on a punishment.

"We all got in trouble." Vee pitched her neatly stamped pile in the bin.

"And for punishment, being together in air-conditioning for two weeks is a whole lot better than pulling weeds from the community center's flower beds, like my mom wanted us to do," Esther said, slapping a book with the stamp. "I'm glad my parents said I could be punished with you three instead. So why are you acting like it's the end of the world?"

"I am not in trouble before." Her English sounded wrong. A single tear splashed on the dusty cover of an oversized picture book.

"Never?" chorused three astonished voices.

Shaking her head, Aneta set down the book. "I disappoint Mom and The Fam." Her English worsened when she was going to cry. *What if they send me back?* But she didn't tell the girls. They wouldn't understand.

"We were stupid." Sunny straightened and stared at her dirty hands. "We got excited about a Crocs Killer clue. Now we're stamping discarded books at the library to be thrown in the Dumpster. How lame is that, stamping books that will be thrown out?"

"But speaking of the Crocs Killer. . ." Vee looked up with a gleam in her eye.

"And catching her. . ." Esther dropped another book in the bin and stepped alongside Aneta, patting her arm.

"Let's go over what we know," Vee said. "How long do you think they'll keep us here?"

Esther shrugged. "You're right, Vee. We can't go ahead with an investigation without knowing where we are."

Both Vee's brows shot up.

"It *is* a good idea to see what we know," Esther insisted.

The heat in Aneta'a face receded, and she smiled a watery smile. "Right."

Sunny leaned against the metal counter and took her water bottle out of her backpack. She gulped twice then recapped the bottle. "We think she had to come down from the community center because we saw her through the trees, remember?"

Esther hoisted herself on the counter. "And since she came from here, someone might have seen her. Somebody carrying a wriggling garbage bag is *not* something you see every day." Esther tugged at the waist of her capris. "At least not in the library parking lot."

"So." Vee whipped out her tiny notebook and flipped to a new page. "Interview people at the community center, the library, and the senior center." She groaned. "That's a lot of interviewing."

Esther rolled her eyes. "Do you always have to do that?"

Vee ignored her. "What did everyone see? Let's start with that."

"I don't remember anything. After Wink yelped, it all got really terrible." Esther shrugged. "Aneta jumped off the dock, I pushed the boat into the water, and you ran for help."

"And I stood there shrieking at the woman," Sunny said. "Sorry, guys."

Aneta thought hard. What *had* she seen? "The woman wore shorts," she said slowly. "Dark."

"She had her back to me, headed for the lake. I never saw her face." Sunny scrunched her eyes. "All I saw was the white wriggling bag and"—she snapped her fingers—"and a hat! She was wearing a cap with a brim. It was khaki!"

"Some brand name on it," Vee added thoughtfully. "I remember that. Before I ran." Vee read from her notebook. "Dark shorts. Khaki hat with logo. That's a start."

"I think the next thing we need to do is—" Esther stepped forward. At that moment, Gram walked through the doorway, pulling her helmet off. "I've been sent to spring the prisoners," she said, sounding like a tough guy.

"You mean we're free?" Sunny dropped the stack of books she'd been working on. "Yowch!" Hopping on one foot, she clutched her other sneakered foot. "For today or forever? Ouch—right on my foot!"

"Forever. I called all your parents. They agreed you could be released into my custody. Going onto Mr. Leonard's backyard was a mistake. I think you girls realize that and know trespassing is wrong. And"—her gaze took in the full bins—"I think you've served your time. I've brought the Scooter Patrol to transport."

Zeff entered, a frown on his tanned face. Uncle Luke followed close behind with a big wave at the girls. Laura, Zeff's twin and a foot shorter than her brother, peeked around him. She waved. She was home after a summer internship. Zeff held up one of the Dog Waddle posters. Seeing the drawing of Wink reminded Aneta about the Crocs Killer clues. A woman with dark shorts and a khaki hat could be *anyone* in Oakton.

"Where did you get the poster?" Vee asked as she stamped the last book in her pile.

"It's coming back," Zeff said. He thrust the poster at Sunny. Then he pulled three more out of his messenger bag. Looking over at Aneta, he shrugged. "I'm sorry, 'Neta. All these businesses stopped me as I ran my courier route. Said they wanted nothing to do with the Dog Waddle." His hand reached into the bag once again, this time withdrawing two more. "Some girl gave me these. Said she'd gotten them from business owners who said no way to the Dog Waddle."

The stunned silence was brief.

"A girl?" Esther snapped out the words, her face reddening. She surveyed the others. "Melissa Dayton-Snipp."

Vee nodded grimly. "Has to be."

Sunny smacked her hand into her palm and made a hideous face. "She's not going to get away with her Operation Ditch Dog Waddle. We'll stop her evil plan!"

Chapter 12

Piles of Puppy Pellets

I do not understand!" Aneta yelled into the summer heat, arms wrapped around Gram's waist as the pink scooter waited at a traffic light. She glanced over her shoulder and grinned at the scooters behind: Zeff with Sunny, Uncle Luke with Esther, and Laura with Vee hanging on.

Gram tipped her head toward Aneta. "Understand what?" she called back.

"Why Melissa hates Wink."

The light changed, and Gram placed her feet on the foot treads and twisted the right grip accelerator. Over her grandmother's shoulder, Aneta watched the dial climb to thirty-five miles per hour.

"She doesn't hate Wink!" Gram shouted. "She doesn't. . ." The wind tore a few words away. ". . .jealous. . .an idea that people like better than hers!"

Aneta understood the bits of words. She hugged her grandmother. People did like their idea. Just yesterday, when Mom and Aneta had walked to The Sweet Stuff, several people had stopped them to say how much they were looking forward to the Waddle. One man said his sister was coming in from Ohio with her basset hound. Mom beamed as though Aneta had come up with the idea all herself.

At least people had liked their idea until Melissa had started this trouble. Once the girls had signed out of the library, Gram had suggested they cruise Main Street to see which businesses no longer had posters.

"I'm sure these business owners misunderstood Melissa," Gram had said, a glint in her eye. Aneta knew that look. Each store owner would be treated to the Jasper negotiation skills. *Negotiation* was one of the first English words Aneta had learned. Well, at least Gram and the rest of the family had the Jasper negotiation skills. Despite the laughing encouragement of The Fam to "never say, 'Oh, okay,' " when a discussion was needed, Aneta still caved when someone said, "This is the way it's going to be."

She was so lost in thinking about her lack of Jasper-ness that she forgot to watch for Wink-less storefront windows until a high-pitched beep of a scooter behind them startled her back to their mission. Gram glanced at her rearview mirror on the handlebars, signaled, eased over to the curb, and parked diagonally.

After Aneta swung her leg off the scooter and removed her helmet, she waved at the three girls, who had also dismounted. Sunny gestured to the big glass window with the words PETE'S PETS EMPORIUM. "What's emper-reum?" Aneta asked Gram, who was fluffing her hair.

"Emm–pour–eee–um," Gram pronounced. "A fancy name for a store. Looks like he either got missed with a Waddle poster or he's one of Melissa's victims."

The group converged on the store. Esther was the first to push open the door, and air-conditioned air flowed over them. It felt good, yet Aneta shivered. After the baking heat of the ride, her skin felt like she'd gotten too close to a campfire and now ice cubes.

A man of average height wearing a button-front plaid shirt looked up. He viewed the group without speaking. Then his gaze fell on the drawing of Wink. His face crumbled into unfriendly lines.

"I don't want one of them posters." He stood stiffly, arms straight at his sides.

Before she knew what her legs were doing, Aneta had stepped from behind Gram to the counter. She extended her hand and said, "I'm Aneta. Please tell me why." Although softly spoken, it didn't sound like a question. It sounded like she expected the man to answer her. To her surprise, he did!

"Well. . ." He seemed uncertain, as though he had once known but couldn't quite remember. "It's, um. . ." He paused again then spoke up loudly. "The pollution problem."

"Pollution problem?" Sunny sputtered. Vee yanked her behind Zeff's bulky body.

"Yes," the man said, now speaking more quickly and confidently. "All them dogs doing their business in the park. People won't like it. They'll track it everywhere. It will affect my business."

Having said more than she had ever thought she'd say to a complete stranger, Aneta now stood silent. Everyone knew that dogs went to the bathroom, didn't they? Why would it affect his business?

Vee stepped forward and placed the poster on the counter. The man looked at it and then looked away. She said firmly, "We have volunteers who will scoop poop. Maybe you don't know why we chose the Dog Waddle for our fund-raising project for Oakton Founders' Days?"

The man shifted from one foot to another and rearranged a counter display of catnip toys.

Esther was the next to stand near the counter. Although she didn't lean over toward the man, she placed her neatly painted nails of each hand on the glass top. "It's to help dogs who don't have homes. You own a pet store. I bet you love dogs."

Within the next few minutes, the other three girls had started a tag-team relay of Wink stories, as well as what Nadine had told them about Paws 'N' Claws Animal Buddies' rescue efforts. The man stood frozen. Aneta hid a smile. She wouldn't know what to do either if those three girls were talking that fast to her.

As the girls carried on, Aneta heard several yips. Turning her head toward the sound, she noticed the corner of a wire pen sticking from behind a pile of Puppy Pellet dog food, stacked about waist high. With nothing to add to the very capable job the girls were doing, Aneta wandered away from the counter toward the wire pen. Bags of Puppy Pellets lay haphazardly stacked six high on three sides of the pen.

"Oh!" Aneta gasped. "Little Winks!"

The pen held six basset puppies; two lay on their sides, flanks heaving as though they were too hot. Two more rose to their feet but didn't approach Aneta. They looked tired. "Poor babies. Are you hot, too?" She glanced at an overturned water bowl. "No water, huh? I will get you some." A bunch of Winks who needed help. The last two bassets in the pen, however, stopped tugging on a dirty towel and watched her, tails looping up like question marks. Together, with their big feet stepping squarely on their long ears, they stumbled across the pen toward Aneta.

Distracted from the water mission, she dropped to her knees, leaning against the pile of Puppy Pellets. "So cute," she murmured. She couldn't wait until Wink was at her home. She hoped all these puppies would find forever homes, too. Funny how there were so many bassets about Wink's size. She stuck her fingers through the wire pen.

"Hi, puppies."

At the same moment, the two stumblers collided with the pen and promptly sank sharp puppy teeth into her wriggling fingers.

"Ouch!" She jerked her fingers away. The action pushed her against a bag out of order in the stacking. One began to slowly slide. Aneta fell farther backward, kicking the pen with her flailing feet while she tried to balance herself.

"Whoa!" she cried.

"Ai-ai!" the puppies cried.

The dislodged bag pushed the one nearest it out of the stack. The entire wall of Puppy Pellets cascaded toward Aneta's head. She pushed at the bags, but they were too big, too heavy, and gaining speed.

"Help!" she cried, throwing up her arms to ward off the heavy bags. They pushed her over, and faster than the breath to cry out, she lay half-buried in dog food. The yelping puppies increased their volume. Her cheek hurt from scraping the cement floor.

"Oh, ow." She opened her eyes. "Help." The logo of the bag scrunching her nose looked familiar. *Later,* Aneta thought. *I will think about it later when I breathe.*

Chapter 13

A Clue to the Crocs Killer!

*D*azed, she heard the girls approaching. "Aneta! He's going to put the poster back up. Aneta? Aneta!"

Esther shrieked. "Aneta! Lord, help her!"

Yes, please, Lord, Aneta thought, speaking to Him for the first time. Her cheekbone began to throb in beat with other parts of her body awkwardly twisted under too much puppy food. Puppy Pellets did not smell good. Especially when one of the bags had split open and she was nearly swimming in Pellets. Some were in her ear. Trying to push herself up while everyone pulled off bags, several Pellets crushed under her elbow.

Finally, she was free of Puppy Pellets. The girls helped her up and brushed her off. All but two of the puppies, still delighted at the entertainment, had settled down to a lower-voiced grunting and grumbling. The quiet pair raised their heads briefly, appearing too tired to care.

The pet-store man pushed past Gram and the girls to regard the mess. "I hope you're not thinking to sue me," he said to Aneta, who was touching her pulsating cheekbone. "You owe me for forty pounds of Puppy Pellets!"

How much does forty pounds of Puppy Pellets cost? Aneta felt her face grow hot, hot, hot. Her Christmas money was long gone. "I am sorry," she said, backing up. Zeff's long arm slipped around her. She leaned against him. "I heard the puppies. They did not have water. One of them bit my finger. I jerked my hand back. It hit one of the bags. I fell."

Cousin Zeff cleared his throat. "Good thing it was you, Aneta, and not one of those tiny little pups." He inspected the two remaining walls of Puppy Pellets. He nudged one with his toe. That side began to slide. With a quick move, Zeff stopped them from tipping over the wire pen. "Anything could have tipped them over to squash the puppies."

The pet-store man shook his head. "You dog people."

Aneta found that curious. Wasn't he a dog person if he owned a pet store?

Zeff reached for his wallet, gazing at the two quiet puppies, the overturned water dish, and the dirty towel. "I'll pay for the food," he said. "No problem. Then I'll come back later today and expect to find this pen clean and the water fresh." He pointed to the quiet puppies. The lawyer tone Aneta knew well entered his voice. "They look sick. What kind of place are you running here?"

The lawyer tone ran in each of The Fam's voices. Except hers. Each of The Fam were involved somehow in making things right. Gram's husband and Aneta's grandfather, "Grand," was overseas right now, helping a refugee agency deal with some legal thing. Zeff attended college to become another Jasper lawyer. Laura volunteered as a victim's advocate. Uncle Luke was a retired policeman. He now stepped toward the front of the group.

"There's not a problem, is there?" he asked mildly. With his short gray hair, Hawaiian shirt, and his big chest that made it hard for his arms to lay flat against his body, he looked like a private detective in a movie. No matter what he wore, everyone listened to Uncle Luke.

Now the pet-store man's tone changed from mad to fake nice. "Not a problem. It's just been busy here this morning. These pups just arrived, and then you folks came and I wasn't able to come back and check on them. Our puppies are well taken care of."

After making sure Aneta wasn't bleeding anywhere and suggesting a stop at the The Sweet Stuff for an ice bag for the cheekbone and a caramel sundae for her tears, Gram ushered the group toward the front.

The girls petted the puppies one last time. Esther ran to get fresh water. Near the front door, Gram favored the pet-store owner with a big smile. "Thank you so much for putting the poster back up." She eyed the poster on the counter. "You will be putting the poster back up? Today?"

"Okay, okay," he said, throwing up his hands. "I'll put the poster back up."

"And keep it up and in a highly visible place until the day of the Oakton Founders' Days Dog Waddle?"

His eyebrows slanted over his narrowed eyes while his shoulders slumped. Aneta marveled at how her grandmother had known the man had no intention of keeping his promise. Gram was amazing.

He sighed. "Yeah."

"Great," Gram continued in a voice that sounded as sweet as a warm baked peanut-butter cookie. "I walk, run, or scooter past here at least once a day. I'll be happy to see the poster each time

I pass your store." The emphasis on *each time I pass your store* was unmistakable.

Once they were all by the curb and the scooters, Vee wrinkled her nose. "I don't like that place. It smelled so bad. I know dogs do their business in there, but shouldn't he clean it up right away?"

Gram, Uncle Luke, and the cousins were tossing glances back and forth. Aneta watched them. *What do they know that we do not?* Aneta thought of the puppies and the Puppy Pellets that had trapped her. Gingerly, she touched her cheek. Then her hand flew to her mouth. The bags. *Puppy Pellets.*

"A clue!" she whispered, staring at Sunny, who was watching her with a question in her blue eyes. Vee and Esther gathered around her. Gram and the cousins stood behind. "The Puppy Pellets! It is a clue to the Crocs Killer!"

Esther wrinkled her brow. "There wasn't any dog food by the lake that day."

"No." Aneta laced her fingers into a tepee and pressed them to the neckline of her turquoise shirt. "The Crocs Killer wore hat with Puppy Pellets sign on it! I see them on the wall near the Puppy Pellet display." Again her English was botched, but she didn't care.

Cousin Zeff shook his head. "She could have gotten it anywhere."

Vee whipped out her notebook and clicked her pen. "No, I saw that same hat display. It had a sign on it that said, 'Exclusive commemorative hat for our favorite Frequent Buyer customers.' Something like the twenty years Puppy Pellets had been in business or something."

"Something about frequent-buyer customers got the hat," volunteered Uncle Luke, squinting up into the sky as though his memory were up there. "Now I remember, too."

"I say we go back and ask the man if he knows anyone who wears that kind of hat," said Esther, placing her hands on her hips.

"Uh, I don't think that man wants to tell us *anything* now," Sunny said.

Aneta wrinkled her face. "I make him mad by tipping over the Puppy Pellets." She patted her bruised cheek.

"He wasn't happy with us before that," Gram said, her mouth tightening. "He just wanted us out of there. Did you notice the entire time we were by the puppies, he acted awfully nervous?"

"Yeah, and awfully annoyed for a spilled bag of cheap dog food," Zeff said.

"You know what the hat and the Puppy Pellets promotion means." Vee flipped the notebook shut and returned the pen to her pocket. Her eyes widened.

Esther rolled her eyes. "Don't keep us in suspense, Vee. What does it mean other than people who wear the hats buy a lot of Puppy Pellets?"

"It means," Vee said smugly, tapping the pen against her chin, "there's more than Wink at the Crocs Killer's place."

Chapter 14

What Is Melissa Up To?

Sitting on wire chairs next to glass-topped wire tables outside The Sweet Stuff, the girls savored enormous balls of ice cream on crispy waffle cones, compliments of Uncle Luke. Esther sighed happily, licking a stray dribble before it reached her thumb. "Melissa tried to ruin it for us, but she didn't win. Now we just have to do a great job at the Waddle tomorrow."

"We will," Vee said confidently, efficiently devouring her two scoops of plain vanilla ice cream.

"We got all the posters put back up and even added two stores we'd missed!" Sunny tipped her head and lapped around the edge of her cone to catch the quickly melting scoops of bubble gum and cake batter. "I think I'm going to recite our little speech in my sleep."

"You mean this?" Aneta, over her giggles, recited in very good English: "Hi, we'd like to know why you took down the Dog Waddle poster. We'd like to help you feel more comfortable about this important fund-raiser for Oakton's Paws 'N' Claws Animal Buddies." It had been Gram's idea to add "feel more comfortable."

The girls applauded one-handed, other hands clutching their treats. "You were right, Mrs. Jasper, to tell us that we should ask them for their reasons. They couldn't give us even one. I think most of them were embarrassed that they listened to Melissa. The only thing we got as a suggestion was to make sure there were dog-doo-doo cleanup bags." Vee looked at Gram with respect and raised her double scoop in salute. "Good thing the IFA store had already donated a bazillion dog cleanup bags. People liked that we already had pooper-scoopers."

"That volunteered to dress up and dance while they worked," Gram added. "Very cool."

"My youth group is very cool," Esther said.

"I just might come to your very cool youth group sometime," Vee said. When Esther's eyes widened, Vee quickly continued, "Might. I said might."

"I will come. C.P. says I will have a very great time and learn about God as a forever home," Aneta said.

"Really." Gram looked thoughtful. "Forever home. Hmm."

"I am worried about the other Winks." Aneta leaned back in her chair. "Our Waddle will be great. Mom will fall in love with Wink and his secret costume. Then she will want to adopt him. But what about the other dogs where Wink was?"

Esther shot her a quizzical look. "You said the very first day we rescued him you were adopting Wink. Your mom hasn't said yes *yet?*"

Aneta peeped a glance at Gram, who was licking her mocha cone as though she wasn't paying attention to the conversation. Aneta knew better. Part of why she knew better was that Cousin Laura had shot Gram a look and kicked her under the table.

"Um. . ." Aneta squirmed and took another lick. *If only I had*

*not bragged I would adopt Wink. I thought it would be so easy to ask
Mom and have her say yes.*

"Uh-oh." Sunny looked past Aneta's shoulder toward the
patio door of The Sweet Stuff. "Here comes Melissa."

Esther muttered, "I bet she's not too happy about those
posters being back up."

"Get ready, folks," Sunny said quietly. "Drama is in the
house!"

Melissa walked directly to Gram, ignoring the girls, and
offered her hand. "Hello, Mrs. Jasper." Gram shook it.

Vee said, "Hi, Melissa. Seen all the Waddle posters for
tomorrow?"

*Oh, Vee. She said that so Melissa would know we know what
she did,* Aneta thought. She wished she could come up with
something fast like the girls did. The girls were more like The
Fam than Aneta. The Fam had big brains, big mouths, and big
hearts, Grand always said. Aneta wished she did. But, on the
other hand, it was never a good idea to make Melissa mad. Ever.

"I treated the girls. Would you like to join us?" Uncle Luke
said.

Four pairs of eyes whipped around to glare at him. Aneta
choked on the last bit of the crunchy cone. You never knew what
Uncle Luke might do. Ever.

Melissa smoothed her shirt over her capris. "Oh, thank you
very much. I like The Sweet Stuff like the girls do." She shifted
her attention to Esther's T-shirt, the slogan HIS PAIN YOUR GAIN
stretching across the girl's round stomach. Esther squirmed, and
Melissa continued, "Of course, I can't eat here much. I'd get fat."

Esther's eyes began to glitter with tears.

"Hey," muttered Zeff, his heavy brows slamming together.

Cousin Laura slowly raised her head from where she'd been checking her phone. She surveyed Melissa from under equally heavy and equally unhappy brows. She pursed her lips. Any moment she was going to say something Jasper-ish.

"Melissa, why you tell people to take down Wink's poster?" Aneta asked, feeling a heat rise inside. Why was Melissa always so mean?

"Oh, that." Melissa flipped her hand like she was erasing what Aneta said. "I'm sure what you meant to say was 'why *did* I tell people?' Verbs are so hard if you're not an American."

"Oh, for pizza sake!"

Aneta had not seen Sunny's face so red before. She looked like she might shatter into a thousand bits if she heard Melissa say another word. Before Aneta could think about it, she had kicked Sunny under the table. Sunny, startled, shifted her gaze to Aneta. Aneta gave her a "don't" shake of the head. Sunny took a deep breath, stretching her clenched fingers.

"I'm not here to join your party," Melissa said, turning sideways like a model on the runway, ready to strut back behind the curtains. "I'll see you in a few hours."

Puzzled looks all around.

Vee was on her feet. "Why?"

Melissa smiled so wide, all her perfect white teeth showed. She waved the tips of her fingers on her right hand and turned away. The last words floated back. " 'Bye now."

They watched her disappear back through the patio door.

Aneta broke the silence. "Something is bad here."

"Sure thing," Sunny said, leaping up and circling the table. "She's up to something, and it's not good for the Waddle."

Chapter 15

Racing against Time

Half an hour later at the library, Nadine hung up the phone and swiveled her big leather chair toward them. "The council secretary is a volunteer with Paws 'N' Claws. She tells me the people who live on Park Street called the council offices to say they don't want the barking dogs in the park. One lady said she was afraid of vicious dogs. Tonight's a regular council meeting, so somebody put the vote about the Waddle on the agenda."

Wink melted into a puddle of nonvicious basset wrinkles. He rolled his eyes toward Aneta. This meant, "Belly rub, please." She rubbed while sighing. Another obstacle. Her costume idea for Wink was perfect. What if Wink never got to waddle and make Mom fall in love?

"That somebody is probably Melissa's mother." Vee clasped her arms around her skinny knees. The girls were sitting next to Wink's empty pen. Wink dozed off.

"They can't do that. The Waddle is tomorrow!" Sunny cried.

Nadine shrugged. "They can if animal control gets complaints from citizens that they feel the event threatens their safety."

"What would we do with all the Waddlers?"

"It could happen. They could stop us."

"Not necessarily. We can't stop now!"

"It's *tomorrow*, for pizza sake!"

The girls' cries came fast and furious.

"Then you've got to come up with a plan." Nadine tipped her head toward Wink. "That little guy deserves his day to waddle for Aneta's mom."

For long moments, no one said anything. Nadine helped a few children and one parent who came to the desk. Otherwise, the only sounds were the murmurs from library patrons in other parts of the building along with Wink's soft whuffling snores.

Sunny's voice, slow and thoughtful, ended the silence. "Remember Mr. Leonard's garage and how Wink thought it was so fascinating?" She rolled back on the carpet. Wink woke up and hop-stomped over. Flinging his head onto her stomach, he lurched first one front paw and then another up on her side. His right paw trapped his right ear. His rear feet struggled to get a push off the carpet and failed. He wailed. Sunny giggled. "Ouch, Wink. Remember those puppy claws, please." She scooped one hand under his rear end and boosted him onto her. He wobbled and tripped toward her face. More giggles. "Mr. Puppy Breath."

"What does that have to do with Melissa and her plan?" Vee demanded.

Sunny stopped her giggles and frowned, ignoring Vee's comment. "What was in the garage that Wink wanted to check out? What's that high-pitched sound? Why would he need an air conditioner in his *garage*?"

"Well, all I know is that I'm not going there again." Esther uncrossed her legs and lurched to her feet. "Mr. Leonard scares me."

"We need to focus, girls. Don't you want to save the Waddle?" Vee asked them. "I mean, we're going to look pretty stupid if we let everyone down now." She pulled out the notebook and pen. Esther rolled her eyes. "We're going to have to talk to every single neighbor on that street. Including Mr. Leonard. And we have to do it in less than three hours."

"We could just call them, Miss Bossy." Esther jerked her hands to her hips.

A Mom saying came to mind as Aneta watched the two girls square off. Again. "I see thunder on the horizon" meant trouble was coming. Vee and Esther had been friendlier during the past two weeks. Nothing started them up faster, Aneta knew, than Esther not wanting to do what Vee came up with first.

"For one reason, we don't have their phone numbers. And second"—Vee began to write—"we need to do what Aneta's Gram suggested before. That worked. Then have them sign a form that says they are now okay with the Waddle."

"Yes, ask them what we can do to change their minds," Aneta said. "But that is Mr. Leonard's street. Where we got in trouble." Aneta wadded up one of Wink's ears. *Squidgy, squidgy.* That was her made-up word for the wrinkly wads. The puppy half opened his eyes. He loved her to gently squish his ears.

"Yes." Vee stared off into space. "I can't believe we have to do something *else* to keep Melissa from winning."

Esther put her hands on her hips. "You are *obsessed* with winning, Vee, when this is a fund-raiser for a *good cause* that Melissa is trying to *ruin.*"

Vee's gaze fell on her backpack. "Everything is about winning."

"I'm sorry, girls," Nadine interrupted. "You've only got three hours before the meeting. What are you going to do?"

"Three hours!" Sunny yelped. "That Melissa!"

"I'll go to the other four houses, but I'm not going back to Mr. Leonard's." Esther stared each of them right in the eyes.

Aneta shook her head. "It is okay, Esther. You do not have to."

The girls reviewed their plan with Nadine.

She shook her head. "I don't know. It's a long shot. But I have to give you girls credit for trying." She called her friend back at the council. The council said that they could bring the neighbors' approval to the meeting.

While Sunny, Vee, and Esther argued over which house to go to first, and Vee and Esther bickered over who would create the document for the homeowners to sign, Aneta used Nadine's phone to call Mom. She thought it might make the girls happier if there was a sleepover involved after the hot, sweaty work of talking to the neighbors. They would celebrate collecting all the signatures. Mr. Leonard would see that they were truly sorry and only wanted to do a good thing.

While she waited for Mom's assistant to get Mom on the phone, she thought about how Esther didn't seem to like to go home. She always looked for any kind of invite that would mean she could stay longer at Aneta's. Then Mom's voice sounded on the phone.

"Are you all right?"

After Aneta asked about the sleepover, Mom's voice took on a smile. She agreed promptly, saying she'd bring dinner home for all of them. "I'll come home early so you girls can have a swim after your hard work."

After Aneta told the girls about the sleepover, the other three called home. It was a yes for everyone! Then they were off. The signature sheet came off the printer. The clock was ticking: less than three hours to get all five signatures.

"Oh! I thought that lady would never stop showing us pictures of her cats! We've lost so much time!" Vee bit her lip, jumping down the steps of the house next door to Mr. Leonard's. She flourished yet another signature on the form.

"We couldn't be rude. She might not have signed the sheet! Okay, we're down to mean Mr. Leonard's house." Sunny pulled her hair off her neck and fanned herself. "How much time do we have left?"

"Forty-five minutes. Now we won't have time to go to Aneta's house and swim before the meeting." Esther frowned at her watch.

"Silly Cat Woman," Sunny said, twirling around with her arms out. "I am cooking, cooking, cooking in this heat. The pool would be so cooooool!"

"If you'd stop hopping all over the place, you probably wouldn't be so sweaty." Esther's face was redder than Sunny's under the Paws 'N' Claws Animal Buddies cap each of the them had been given by Nadine. "I'll wait under that tree"—she gestured across the street to the park and its perimeter of oak trees—"until you're done with *him*." Without waiting for Vee to answer, she walked across the street.

"She's making a giant deal. He's not that scary," Vee said, her almond eyes narrowing as her gaze followed Esther. "We just have to do what we've done for each of the other four houses."

"Introduce Wink, tell his story, explain the Waddle, and

ask him to sign the document." Aneta had it down. She'd even made the speech at the last house. She was speaking a lot lately. She glanced down at the low-rider puppy nosing up and down her leg like a vacuum cleaner. She laughed as it tickled. It was easier to speak up when it had to do with Wink. Then her smile vanished. She couldn't bear to think of someone else adopting him. The day before, all the posters had only caused Mom to say, "You did a tremendous job with the poster, sweetie. That little dog looks like he could fall right off the paper."

"Might be a good time to ask God if you could have Wink," Sunny said suddenly.

"You mean I should talk to Him like I talk to Mom?" Aneta asked. "A forever home for Wink." C.P.'s comment had stuck in her head.

"Yep," Esther answered. "Now, can we get back to the Waddle?"

Wink's costume in the Waddle was her last hope for Mission Mom. If that meant talking to Mr. Leonard, then she would.

"We'll say we're sorry again about going on his lawn," Sunny said. "Grown-ups like it when you say you're sorry a lot."

Grasping the leash firmly, Aneta marched toward Mr. Leonard's front door. Wink once again leaned into his harness as they passed the driveway leading to the separate garage in back, but she teased him away to follow her.

"What *is* it that he smells over there?" Vee asked, stepping over him as she mounted the steps. She rang the bell; Aneta picked up Wink and joined her. Sunny stood at the bottom of the stairs. The tiny front porch barely held two girls and a squirming puppy. Aneta glanced back; Esther was watching from across the street. Sunny was bouncing up and down on her toes.

Up. And down. Up. And down. The redhead flashed her a smile and gave her a thumbs-up.

Three times Vee pressed the buzzer, and three times no one came to the door. She looked at Aneta. Aneta looked back. Wink whined, and Aneta realized she'd been clutching him too tightly.

"Now what?" Vee asked, her brow arching high.

"Here, let me," Aneta insisted, shifting Wink to her left arm and knocking loudly on the door. Again. And again. Someone had to be home. They had done too much to let Melissa stop them. What about all the dogs that would get help from Paws 'N' Claws Animal Buddies because of the Waddle?

"Ow!" She drew her hand away from the door.

No one came to the door. The two girls looked at each other. Vee shrugged. She reached over and patted Wink. In silence, the two girls walked down the steps as though their feet were weighted with concrete.

Esther crossed the street and joined them. "One crummy signature short," she said. She checked her watch. "We've got to go straight to the meeting. No more time. Vee?"

Vee pulled out the ATP, and each girl called her family. The parents would meet them at the council meeting. The tightness in Aneta's throat threatened to choke her. What would the council do with four signatures?

Sunny had moved to the driveway and was eyeing the garage. Aneta could tell a plan was forming in that curly head. As the group stood forlornly on the sidewalk, she spoke.

"I wonder if there's a car in the garage," she said. "I thought I saw the curtains move upstairs while you rang the bell."

Vee, Aneta, and Esther peered up at the second story where three curtained windows marched across. "Which window?" Vee asked, craning her neck.

"Doesn't matter." Sunny shrugged. "Nobody's answering the door."

"So what are we going to do about the last signature?" Esther looked like she would cry. "Melissa is so mean!" She stamped her foot like she wished Melissa lay under it.

As they crossed the street, Wink wound the leash around their ankles, interrupting the conversation as they tripped over each other. Finally, they had to stop in the middle of the street to untangle themselves from the leash and each other.

"We did our best." Sunny shoved her hands in her pockets. She didn't sound like she believed it. Aneta didn't for sure. Like she had when she pulled Wink from the lake, she wondered. . . had her best been good enough?

Twenty minutes later, the girls stood in front of the council chamber doors. Back to the courtroom-like place. *Will Wink and the rest of the bassets get to waddle? Will Mom get to see his costume and fall in love with him and say yes, come to our forever home?* It would take a miracle to convince the council that four signatures were good enough. *Um, please God, if You could. . .*

Chapter 16

Hooray!

Later that evening, after darkness had enclosed the patio into its circle of twinkle lights around the pool, Mom swept Aneta off her feet in yet another big hug. "I am so proud of you!"

From his reclining position at the pool edge, Cousin Zeff raised his lemonade glass, ice clinking. "You surprised me, little Aneta. Never thought you'd step right up to that mic in the council chambers and say, 'Four signatures *is* good enough.'"

"Why not?" Mom said, her arm still around her daughter's waist. "She's a Jasper."

Gram's smile glowed in the lights. "I e-mailed Grand that you did a great job asking the council to completely approve the Waddle for good!"

"Pretty cool for a tall, skinny girl." C.P.'s voice came from the top of the fence. Aneta looked over and smiled at him. How did the short C.P. manage to hang over the top without falling backward? One of these days she would find out.

"Okay, C.P., come on over. I know you're dying to. And yes, Gram made baba ghanoush." Mom raised the tray she was bringing from the kitchen. The boy's eyes lit up. He disappeared.

She and Aneta returned to the kitchen for yet more food. Where they would find room to put it on the table was anyone's guess. When it came time for dessert, Aneta filled a large blue bowl with sliced strawberries. Mom removed the pail of vanilla ice cream from the freezer then retrieved several boxes of shortbreads from the pantry. Party sounds wafted in from the pool. The Fam and the three girls were all talking at once. Aneta cocked her head to hear, but only picked up snippets: ". . . was awesome. . . Just stood there. . .spoke clear as. . ." A heavy splash interrupted the conversations. Loud squeals followed. Aneta grinned at Mom. Mom winced. "My nephew again with the pool throwing? I hope your new friends don't mind getting wet."

Aneta shook her head, picked up the tray with the strawberries and cookies, and moved toward the french doors. "Esther's the only one who might get mad. I hope he doesn't throw her in."

Two steps later, onto the patio, she witnessed a drenched Esther in the pool, shrieking with glee and attempting to shove Cousin Zeff's head under the water.

By the time The Fam left, it was long dark. The girls got out their sleeping bags from the hall where Vee, Esther, and Sunny had dropped theirs when they arrived.

"Let's put them on the grass over here," Vee suggested, tucking her bag under her arm and striding to the edge of the slate patio.

"No, over here." Esther took her bag to where the door opened into the house. "It's closer to the house, in case—" She paused. "Well, just in case."

Aneta stood between the two girls. She shot a sideways

glance at Sunny. Not tonight. Sunny shrugged and hefted her sleeping bag to her shoulder, following Esther. "No problem. I'll sleep where Esther wants to sleep, and Aneta can sleep with Vee." She speared first Vee then Esther with a mock angry look. "Since we all can't get along. You'd think by now we'd have had enough adventures to be a squad. As in *united*."

"Squad?" Aneta liked the sound of that. It sounded like adventure. Like their adventure of rescuing Wink and organizing the Waddle to help others like him. Even adventures of stopping Melissa. "What is the name of our squad?"

Sunny shrugged. "Well, it certainly wouldn't be the Harmony Squad, would it?"

Esther flushed, picked up her sleeping bag, and walked over to where Vee had hers. "If you put it like that. . ." She smiled at the taller girl.

The corners of Vee's mouth turned upward, and she darted forward to deliver a quick hug to Esther. "Yes! Squad member." Then she dashed over to the circular patio table, whipped out her notebook and pen, and began scribbling quickly.

Curious, Aneta stood behind her. Vee had started a list of words, scratching out as many as she wrote.

"What are you doing?" Sunny plopped into the chair to Vee's left while Esther took possession of the one on her right.

"Trying to find a name for our squad."

Esther grinned. "Like maybe the Esther Squad."

Aneta held her breath. Would this be the start of more bickering? But she saw Vee's eyes crinkle in amusement. Aneta let out her breath. Maybe they were starting to. . .like each other?

Vee wrote down each of their names while the other girls watched. Then she ripped three sheets off her notebook and slid them across to Sunny, Esther, and Aneta. "Aneta, three pens, please? We have a *mission* here." She cocked her head at Sunny, who grinned, nodding emphatically.

"Yes. Girls with a mission."

Aneta, pleased there would be no arguing over who led this new project, ran into the house to the junk drawer in the kitchen where she retrieved three pens. Skipping past Mom, who sat in the window seat working on her laptop, she flashed her a smile.

"Having fun, sweetie?"

"Oh, yes!"

"Now," Vee instructed, her eyes alight with excitement after Aneta returned. "See what you can come up with that's a word using our four names. Like the first letter of each of our names, okay?"

Sunny leaped up and twirled. "Yes!" she shouted. "I like this."

Esther said, "That's what brainstorming is all about. Making lots of words and then seeing if there's any worth keeping!"

"Did I make you think this was for a grade? Nope, not for a grade." Another rare Vee smile.

They went to work.

VEAS—from Vee.

VASE—from Sunny.

EAVS—from Esther.

"Okay, that was not easy. I'm the only one who came up with a word," Sunny said.

They regarded their work. Aneta was still staring at her piece of paper. The pen lay next to it.

"Nothing yet?" Sunny asked her.

Aneta shook her head. *S, V, A, E.* They just looked like letters.

"Well, based on what we've got, we're some sort of squad

that does something with flowers and maybe mythical creatures named Veas and Eavs." Esther played around some more with her paper. "I think it was a good idea, Vee, I really do. I just didn't come up with anything."

Vee sighed. "Me neither."

A slight pause then Aneta picked up her pen and wrote the four letters once more. She pushed the paper toward the middle of the table. The other three leaned forward.

"S.A.V.E.," read Vee. Her eyes flew wide. "Aneta! You're brilliant!"

Sunny spun. "I love it."

Esther frowned at the paper. "It is. . . ," she said slowly. Then she looked at Aneta. "You've got the letters of our first names *and* it spells what we are doing for Wink and the dogs." She sniffed. "I might cry."

Aneta giggled, Sunny gave a snort of laughter, and Vee let go with one of her crooked smiles. Esther tipped back her head and laughed hard. "We are the S.A.V.E. Squad!"

C.P.'s face popped up over the fence. "The *what?*" he asked, gazing with disappointment at the empty patio table.

Esther waved the paper. "We are the S.A.V.E. Squad!"

"You're just lucky girls who get to eat all the time," was his only response as his head disappeared behind the fence.

How does he do that?

Sometime later, Aneta yawned and surveyed the faces of the three girls who had become her friends as well as the S.A.V.E. Squad. Esther and Vee were going through the final checklist for the

Basset Waddle the next morning, while Sunny endlessly skipped around the pool. Aneta glanced at the updated list.

- *The Hound costume kicks off the start.*
- *Sunny has the air horn to blast off the beginning of the Waddle.*
- *Pooper-scoopers at the park & behind the Waddle—Esther make sure they are coming.*
- *Crowns at my house for King and Queen of the Waddle.*
- *Thank-you notes for the judges.*
- *Esther's dad's friend—truck bed at park tonight.*
- *Tell Melissa how much we made.*

She nudged Vee and pointed at the last item. "Mean."

Vee looked like she might argue. Aneta sincerely hoped she would not. Then Vee pushed her hand through her hair and crossed out the last item.

"Only because you're a S.A.V.E. Squadder and—" She swallowed. "You're right."

"Let's swim!" Aneta said. They had special permission tonight since they were a group. She didn't have to say it twice. The girls raced each other into the house to change into their still-wet suits and leaped into the pool—one, two, three, four. Aneta dove down to touch the drain like she always did.

Tomorrow would be the last chance for her to get Mom to fall in love with Wink. Nadine had promised to bring Wink to the park early so he could get into his costume, and she'd okayed Aneta taking care of him all day.

The girls were flinging a beach ball from one to another, and she joined in, bumping up the ball when it came near her. Soon it had changed into a crab crawling contest in the shallow end with shouts of laughter. Esther was very good at crab crawling. Soon Aneta's face ached from smiling. She hoped her smile would be even bigger tomorrow.

Nearly an hour later, Mom stepped through the doorway. "Hey, girls, you must be wrinkled as prunes. *The Dog Dictionary* show is on. Want to come in and watch?"

The Dog Dictionary show, featuring "everything dog from A to Z," was a favorite with Sunny and Esther as well. Vee remarked her stepbrothers, the Twin Terrors, were loyal fans. The girls sprawled on the long leather sofa facing the screen attached to the wall above a stone fireplace. The evening had cooled enough that they opened the french doors to feel the breeze sweeping through. Mom had just left the room when the opening credits ended and the announcer, with his New Zealand accent that Aneta loved, began the segment:

"It could be in your city, your town. Even across your street. Pet owners who try to make money from their dogs. They don't know what they're doing, and it's not a good thing."

The girls were riveted. With the first hidden-camera footage of a room with stacked cages with pans underneath, Aneta's eyes widened. Out of the corner of her eye, she saw Sunny gulping. Vee twisted her fingers. Esther pulled on her earrings.

In the next few minutes, Aneta had learned that making mother dogs have more than one litter a year for several years is unhealthy. Such irresponsible breeding is not allowed in many towns and cities. These dogs didn't get to run around. They spent their lives in a cage having puppies, who also didn't get to run around. Puppies were often sold before they should have left their mothers. She thought about leaving Mom ever. A tear trickled down her cheek.

To get around the rules, backyard breeders were shipping or delivering dogs to pet stores who didn't ask for breeding records, bloodlines, or anything else to ensure the puppies they were selling were healthy. To reduce or eliminate the barking and whining, some backyard breeders had installed kennel-barking devices that silenced the dog with a painful high-frequency sound when it barked. Hidden cameras showed air-conditioning units kept the rooms too cool for puppies but diffused the smell of dog waste not cleaned up promptly.

At the end, Aneta pointed the remote to the TV and clicked. No one said a word. Vee rolled her pen back and forth between her fingers. "Do you remember that high-pitched sound the day we went to Mr. Leonard's yard?"

Chapter 17

Climbing the Fence

Sunny slowly sat up, her freckled face troubled. "Are you going to say what I think you're going to say?"

Esther straightened, blinking quickly. "My aunt has air-conditioning in her house. Mr. Leonard had the same type of machine outside his—" She paused then whispered, "Not outside his house. Outside the *garage*."

Aneta's brain whirled. Wink pulling his sturdy body toward that house. Like maybe he *remembered* it? Or was it simply his extra-efficient nose had sniffed out other dogs?

Sunny smacked her fist into her palm. "We have to go there. Get evidence." She looked out at the darkness over the patio and the pool. "Now."

The other three all talked at once:

"We can't; we've been banned from there."

"My mom said I should have known better than to trespass."

"If I get in trouble again, Mom might send me back."

The girls swung around to Aneta.

"What?" Esther asked as though Aneta had suggested she

should cut off her arm to lose weight.

It was too late to take back those words. Mom and The Fam had said on the day of the court date that she was a Jasper now. Would always be. But what if Aneta getting into trouble made it too difficult for Mom to keep her?

"I do not want to get sent back and not be a Jasper." Her mouth twisted, and her eyes felt like they were on fire. She closed her eyes. She heard the squeak of the leather sofa and felt the shifting weights of the girls around her. She opened her eyes.

"I think I know how you feel, kinda," Vee said in a low voice, her gaze fixed on Aneta. "When my parents got divorced, I thought if I did anything wrong, they'd send me to the other house and if I messed up there, I was out of places."

Vee, so confident, like she had everything planned out all the time, felt afraid like Aneta?

"I can tell you that you've already got your forever home," Sunny said, her chapped hands clasping Aneta's and squeezing. "The Fam is not going to let you go. They're crazy about you."

Esther bobbed her head in agreement.

Sunny leaped to her feet. "We have to leave now. There's no time to be lost. Who even knows if Mr. Leonard suspects us or thinks we're just nosy kids?"

Vee nodded and tucked her notebook and pen into her back pocket. "I agree." She glanced toward the wide doorway to the hall. "How will we get out so no one hears us?"

"Why don't we ask Mom if she can take us? She's a lawyer," Aneta said.

All three stared at Aneta.

"Aneta, you have something to learn about parents." Sunny patted Aneta's arm like an old grandma. "They aren't really big on adventure. Especially, um, nighttime adventures. They'll say we have no proof."

"Yet," Vee inserted.

"Yet," Sunny repeated. "That's what we're going for. *Then* we can tell our parents. They'll tell us what to do next."

Sunny walked over and poked Esther on the shoulder. "You're quiet."

The short girl blew out a long wobbly breath that sounded as though it had been stuffed in her a long time. "I'm not going."

"Why not?" Aneta asked.

"Because we shouldn't prowl around Mr. Leonard's garage in the dark. I think we should tell Aneta's mom," Esther said firmly.

"Okay." Vee jumped into bossy mode. "You stay here. We don't have time to argue about this." She headed toward the patio door. Standing on the threshold, the slight breeze blowing her nearly dry ponytail, she turned back. "Ready, girls?"

Sunny looked at Esther and then at Vee. "Oh boy, I bet I'm going to regret this," she muttered but walked out the patio doorway past Vee. "I guess we go over the fence? If C.P. can do it, so can we."

Vee glanced at the miserable Esther, who was pulling so hard on one earring Aneta was afraid she'd pull her ear off. "Are you going to tell on us?"

Esther bit her lip. Vee made a disgusted sound and a beeline for the fence. "If anyone's coming, now's the time." She moved a patio chair to the fence, hopped up on it, and jumped up until her hands caught the top. Knees squeaking on the vinyl fence, she was up and over. Sunny, slower, but not by much, was next.

Aneta was torn. The sooner they could solve the mystery of who tried to murder Wink, the sooner Mom would see that he needed a Jasper forever home. If she stayed here. . . She hugged Esther. "Please do not tell." Then she walked resolutely over to the chair and fence.

Chapter 18

Stupid in a Group

The plan was simple. Once over the fence, they'd run through the park and into Mr. Leonard's yard. There they would snap pictures of the Puppy Pellets, the hat, and lift Vee—the lightest—up to the garage window. Her ATP camera would capture the evidence. Aneta trotted along with them, the evening air heavily sweet yet disapproving. It had not cooled to the normal night temps. She thought of Mom sleeping, thinking the girls were talking all night on the patio, not knowing that they were running in the dark. Across a darkened park. To a darkened house—without permission. She shivered in spite of the warm breeze.

"Oh no!" Vee stopped short and clapped her hand to her shorts pocket. "My phone!"

"What? Did you forget to charge it?" Sunny asked. She sounded a little breathless and bent over with her hands on her knees. The shortest of the three, she had struggled to keep pace.

"No," Vee cried. "I forgot to *bring* it! It was poking me when we were watching TV, so I took it out of my pocket and put it on the coffee table."

For a moment, Sunny and Aneta could only stare at Vee. Her bleak face stared right back. Aneta crossed her arms, rubbing her elbows. This plan had seemed perfect on the patio. *Now what?*

"Think, think, think. We can't waste time." Sunny blew out a breath and glanced past Vee. "Uh-oh." She quickly looked at the ground. "Don't look over there, but there's a creepy white van slowing down on the side of the park."

Aneta and Vee, of course, turned toward the van.

"I said, *don't* look!"

"Creepy," Vee said. "Let's get out of here."

"Run!" Sunny said. "We'll think on the way!"

Aneta dug in her sneakers and dashed off toward their goal. Whoever the van driver was, she hoped he or she was not interested in three stupid girls up in the night without parents.

"Aneta!" Vee and Sunny's screech stopped her. She looked back. She stood alone in the middle of the street in front of Mr. Leonard's house. Vee and Sunny were nearly at the opposite edge, closest to running home. They were gesturing wildly. "You're going the wrong way! *This* way!"

The van had disappeared.

When Aneta reached the girls, the two took off running again. She had to put on extra speed to catch up. Sunny was gasping out ideas.

"Vee—*gasp-gasp*—you're the fastest." She swallowed, stumbled on a curb, flailed, and righted herself. "Get over the fence, get the phone, get back over the fence." Sunny finally stopped. "I gotta rest." Aneta, while not winded, was relieved.

"Where are you two going to be?" Vee asked, not breathing even a little hard.

"Right behind you," Sunny said. "You meet us, we'll turn around. We've gone this far getting into trouble."

Aneta nodded. "When we show Mr. Leonard is bad, we will not get in trouble." She bit her lip. "Maybe." It was both scary and kind of thrilling—this being out in the middle of the night without parents. She tipped back her head; the stars were out with a quarter moon. The Fam had taken her on the first family field trip to the Oakton Observatory after she became a Jasper. A memory she had tucked away then as the best day of her life. After tonight, she hoped she got to *stay* a Jasper.

With Plan B in place, they ran once more. Once she began gasping, Aneta realized she was forgetting to breathe, so conscious was she not to make any noise that might wake up the neighbors. C.P.'s bedroom window was open and his light on as they quietly jogged across his front yard to the fence. What was he doing up so late? Eating, probably.

As Sunny predicted, Vee made the fence just ahead of them. With one smooth motion that told Aneta Vee had climbed many fences before, the dark-haired girl was on the top, had turned around, and was preparing to drop down when a familiar grown-up voice that was *not* Esther's came out of the darkness.

"Where are the other two, Vee?"

Chapter 19

Banished?

Parents crowded the living room.

Aneta watched Sunny, Esther, and Vee's parents stand with them while Mom paced the front of the room. Mom had never acted this way. They would need to buy gobs of peanut butter. Aneta had shamed Mom—made her look like a bad mom.

A weight like the entire city of Oakton pressed on Aneta. She had already cried and now attempted to keep from breaking into fresh tears. It wasn't working; the tears were rolling silently down her cheeks anyway. How long would it take Mom to decide that Aneta was trouble and send her back? From the looks on the faces of the other parents, they were as unhappy as Mom.

They had already gone through how dangerous it had been to go out alone. "*Stupid* is what it was," Sunny's dad had said. "So was sending Vee back alone. What were you thinking?"

"We were right behind her," Sunny protested. "At least we were stupid in a group. Does that count?" From Sunny's dad's expression, Aneta knew it didn't. The large-panel van slowing down as it passed them at the park rushed back into her mind.

She agreed with Mr. Quinlan.

"We were stupid," she said, raising her eyes to meet his. "I am very sorry we did not think better."

"Well." He didn't seem to know what to say.

"Don't think you're off the hook, Esther, because you didn't go. You should have told Aneta's mother the girls had left. They could have been. . . Well"—Esther's mother glanced at her husband—"a lot of things could have happened." Esther flushed a dull red.

Both of Vee's parents were there; her mother with her new husband and Vee's father with his wife. It was double trouble for Vee, thought Aneta. She only had Mom to look at her so disappointed. Her shame deepened.

The parents left the girls to confer in the kitchen.

"That's not good that they are talking together," Vee said. Her face was pinched, and there were circles under her eyes.

Aneta yawned. It was nearing midnight. "Why?" she asked.

Sunny answered before Vee. "Because it means they'll come up with a punishment for all four of us as well as—"

Esther finished Sunny's sentence, "—as well as getting punished individually by our own parents for getting them out of bed to come here and find us in trouble."

Aneta's gaze moved between the three girls. "How do you know this?"

Each girl shrugged.

Sunny replied, "Practice."

"Will they ground us all?" Vee wondered, her brows nearly touching each other.

"What about the Waddle tomorrow?" Aneta cried.

Esther hissed, "They're coming."

The nine parents reentered the room. The girls faced them. Mom spoke like Aneta imagined she did in the courtroom. "We have agreed that the Waddle is a community project that needs you four girls."

Aneta felt relief.

"So you will be there tomorrow—to help others."

Four whooshes of pent-up breath. Aneta squeezed Sunny's hand. Sunny squeezed back.

Mr. Nguyen stepped forward. Although his words were for all the girls, he never took his gaze off his daughter. She stared at her feet. "However, after that, you four are restricted from seeing each other. Between antagonizing Mr. Leonard by going into his yard and now this, we think"—he gestured toward the parents standing together—"your being together is not a good thing for a while."

Vee's head shot up.

Esther gasped. "Banished?"

Sunny sent a pleading look toward her mother. Aneta could only stare at Mom. They had just become the S.A.V.E. Squad! It was not fair! Two months ago, she had wanted nothing but *out* of the group. Now? She finally had friends. What would it be like without them?

Sunny's parents nodded. The girls held hands. There didn't seem to be anything more to say. Mom broke a silence so thick it stole the air from the room.

"Thank you for coming tonight. Again, I am—so sorry."

Everyone began to move toward the front door. Aneta heard Sunny say to her parents as they passed through the doorway, "Mom and Dad, please forgive me for being an idiot. I'm sorry I disappointed you." Aneta watched both parents embrace their daughter.

When the door closed on the last person, Mom turned to Aneta. Her eyes were red. As she walked toward Aneta and the living room, she rubbed them and sighed. Aneta had thought she would say what Sunny had said to her parents. Instead she threw her arms around Mom. "Please don't send me back. I am sorry I am so much trouble! *Please* don't send me back!"

"Sweetie!" Mom's mouth dropped open. "What are you talking about?"

Once seated on the couch, Mom's arms held her tight. Aneta sobbed until the cries became jerks and gasps. It made her stomach hurt. Mom kept whispering, "Shh, sweetie. Shh. It's all right. You're not going anywhere," until the words began to sink into Aneta's pain.

She raised her head. "You will not send me back?"

Mom shook her head. "Jaspers don't send Jaspers away. I love you so much, Aneta."

Aneta cried all over again. She was still a Jasper. Mom said *always* a Jasper.

"I am sorry I was stupid," she said, wiping her eyes. "I want my forever home here with you and The Fam."

Mom's eyebrows shot up. "Forever home? Sweetie, I love that." She snuggled Aneta. Aneta felt herself drifting into sleep. Did she dream that Mom tucked her in bed like a little girl, whispering, "Tomorrow's the Waddle, my little Jasper, and it will be great"?

Chapter 20

Missing: One Hound Dawg

Aneta knew she wouldn't sleep a wink, what with worrying about Wink, the Waddle, and the upcoming separation from the S.A.V.E. Squad. But then Mom woke her up the next morning and smiled at her.

"French toast, Jasper-style, ready to rumble," Mom said. "Your grandmother brought over a big batch before you were up."

Last night. Aneta's face got hot. "The Fam knows?"

"Are you kidding?" Mom got off the bed and headed for the door. "The Fam has radar for news." She turned at the doorway. "And they don't love you any less, sweetie."

Aneta relaxed then and stretched like a large cat. "I am a Jasper," she said, a smile lighting her face. "Like you. Like The Fam."

"Yes, my delightful daughter, you are. You are also going to be late for the Waddle if you don't get moving." Mom waved from the door, and she was gone. Her voice floated back. "The Fam will meet us at the park."

Aneta jumped out of bed, dressed quickly in shorts and a WAY TO WADDLE T-shirt—designed by her with Esther's help.

Sandals or sneakers? She might have to chase a loose basset at the Waddle. Sneakers. After tying them, she pulled a bulging plastic bag from her dresser, tucked it into her messenger bag, and thudded downstairs.

The two of them ate what Mom called a "gargantuan" breakfast of thick-sliced egg bread stuffed with sweetened cream cheese and then baked in cinnamon honey butter. While they drove the few short blocks to the park, Aneta hid her smiles thinking about Wink in his costume. Mom would fall in love. Aneta would pull him in a wagon that Esther and her brothers and sisters had decorated. Then, when this very last plan worked—and it *had* to—she and Mom would fill out the adoption papers. Paws 'N' Claws Animal Buddies would visit their house and make sure they would be good owners. *Only the best ever.*

She reviewed each girl's job for the day. Vee had the final checklist. Esther would work the sound system for her father, the pastor of the local community church, when he prayed the Blessing of the Hounds. Sunny would shoot off the air horn to signal the beginning of the Basset Waddle. As the girls had worked out, Paws 'N' Claws Animal Buddies would carry out the other details the girls had planned.

The thought of the S.A.V.E. Squad banishment suddenly snuffed out her excitement. She looked through the car window over at Vee, Esther, and Sunny standing next to a Paws 'N' Claws volunteer. Vee had graduated to a clipboard today. Sunny was twirling in excitement around the group. Esther stood with her hands on her hips. Who knew how long the banishment would be? She wouldn't figure out where Vee went with the backpack or hear about the funny things Sunny's brothers said. And who would be Esther's friends?

"You okay, 'Neta?" Mom asked, turning the Lexus into The Sweet Stuff parking lot.

"No," Aneta replied, sniffing, smiling at Mom's abbreviation of her name. The Fam had been great about the whole name thing. "I want to find proof that Mr. Leonard is a bad dog owner. Then the S.A.V.E. Squad banishment would be worth it. Dogs like Wink and the others would at least be safe from Mr. Leonard."

Mom's mouth twitched at *banished.* "I've been thinking about that," she said as the SUV rolled into a parking space. "I called Nadine last night." She looked away, seemed to forget Aneta was there, and murmured, "I must have been crazy." Shaking her head, she looked at Aneta. "After I apologized for waking her up, I explained what you girls think. Now, don't get your hopes up, honey." Mom leaned over to smooth the fly-away strands from Aneta's headband. "Nadine asked her friend, who's a volunteer with Paws 'N' Claws and an animal control officer, to join her and me at the Leonards' in a few minutes."

Hope surged high in Aneta's heart. Mom would make it right. She remembered *The Dog Dictionary* show and the conditions for the dogs. No room for mothers and puppies to move, to develop their legs. Stacks of cages in dark places. Mom would realize that Wink really did need a forever home and the Jasper home was just the one for him. And then maybe the parents would say yes—or at least maybe—to allowing the girls to see each other.

"Thanks, Mom," Aneta said as she climbed out, eager to tell the girls. "I will tell the Squad. You are great."

Mom's eyes got bright. "So are you, Aneta Jasper. I'll see you later, sweetie."

Aneta stepped out of the Lexus. "You must watch the Waddle!" Aneta peered earnestly into the interior of the vehicle. "Wink has a special costume! Promise?"

"Promise. I wouldn't miss it. I can't wait to see your creativity."

"Thank you for calling Nadine." Adjusting her bag over her shoulder, Aneta hurried over to the girls who were waving. Many circular wagging tails and "Aroo! Aroo!" filled the parking lot. She tried to count how many dogs but lost track of which black, white, and brown dog was which, or maybe she had already counted the lemon-and-white gigantic basset, but missed this petite brown and black. She gave up. The count was A LOT. The Waddle would be a success with each of these Waddlers paying both an entry fee and submitting a donation pledge card for Paws 'N' Claws Animal Buddies. The S.A.V.E. Squad had done it.

She told them the news. "Don't get your hopes up." She repeated Mom's admonition.

"Too late," Sunny said. "I'm already thinking we saved Wink's brothers and sisters—if they are all bassets—and that we might get a reprieve from being banished."

"Me, too," Vee and Esther agreed.

Aneta nodded. "Mom's going to call your ATP, Vee, when they are done."

Vee nodded then pointed. "I see the animal control truck now!" The Lexus, Nadine's Toyota, and a brown truck converged on the Leonards' house. "Let's go over the checklist so we don't have to stare at the house and wonder what's going on."

C.P. joined the group with Wink at the end of the red leash. "Nadine told me to give him to you. She's meeting your mom for some secret mission." He handed over the leash. "I wish I had a dog. This guy's cool."

"Why don't you have one?" Vee asked.

"Allergies." C.P. pantomimed great gusty sneezes. The girls backed up.

"Wink doesn't give you allergies?" Kneeling down, Aneta snuggled her face into the soft puppy fur. "Your costume makes Mom fall in love with you," she whispered, kissed him, and moved him to the crook of her right arm so she could dig into the messenger bag. He wriggled mightily; she dropped the bag and bent down to pick it up.

"Not me. My little sister." C.P. shrugged. "So no pets for us. Hope you get Wink so I can visit him."

"In between meals?" Sunny said with a grin. "Will you have time?"

C.P. cupped one hand behind his ear. "Sorry, next time talk into my good ear." He dashed off, his cackling laugh floating back.

"Here," Esther said, removing the puppy from Aneta's arms. "I'll hold him while you get his costume on." She gestured at the covered wagon off to the side. "My sibs helped me decorate it. We had a blast. They want to meet Wink once you've adopted him."

"*If* she gets to adopt him," Vee corrected. Esther's hands shot to her hips. Vee turned her shoulder and surveyed her clipboard. "Wink, costume, and wagon. Check. Sunny"—she turned to the girl who was bouncing on her toes—"you've got the horn to start—"

A Paws 'N' Claws Animal Buddies volunteer rushed up, looking like she'd been grabbing gobs of her hair and twisting. It stood out all over her head.

"The Hound Dawg. Isn't. Here!" she croaked, hands gripped in front of her like she was praying. The long-legged, tricolored basset that wanted very much to sniff Aneta's leg pulled the leash right out of the volunteer's hands to reach his goal. A long line of drool ran down Aneta's leg.

"Oh no!" Esther's voice squeaked. "The Hound is the Squad's coolest idea!"

This was the secret surprise Aneta had told the girls only last week. She and Mom had found a place in the next town over that rented a basset hound costume. Zeff had begged to wear it. When he discovered he was about a foot taller than the costume stretched, however, he roped one of his buddies into being the Hound Dawg. The antics of the Hound Dawg would draw even more people to watch the procession. Esther's family had delivered the plastic tub with the costume to the parking lot with Esther. Aneta scanned the parking lot and then the park. Where *was* the Hound?

"He's supposed to lead the Waddle! What do we do now?" the volunteer said, reclaiming the leash and apologizing for the drool slinging.

Esther looked at Aneta, panic in her eyes. "Call your cousin!" She gestured to Vee's pocket. "Use the ATP!"

Something bumped her back. "Oh, sorry," she said, stepping aside before seeing it was C.P. "Oh, it's you again. You're eating already?"

"Hey, I had breakfast at six thirty with my crazy sister who had to get here to help. I had to come and carry stuff. I'm starving. Want some?" He thrust a still-warm fried dough toward her, butter dripping. Aneta's quick move prevented the glob from landing on her shorts. Wink lunged toward the splotch of grease. It vanished under his long pink tongue. He made a happy puppy face at Aneta. Oh, she loved this little dog.

"C.P., we have an emergency. The Hound Dawg costume is in *here*"—she pointed downward—"and there's no *body* in it."

Stuffing the rest of the treat in his mouth, C.P. wiped his hands on his long shorts. "No problem. I'll wear it." He bent down.

"Um, C.P., you're great to do that, but—"

C.P. lifted the costume from the tub. And lifted and lifted. There was costume as high as he could hold it with significant costume still in the tub. He glanced down then at the girls. His face reddened.

"You're a great guy, C.P.!" Sunny flung an arm around him and with the other hand removed the costume from his hands and dropped it in the tub.

Aneta stepped in to distract C.P. from his embarrassment. She handed over Wink's leash. "Hold Wink. I need to run and find my cousin Zeff. He's here with The Fam. He must call his friend."

"Ten minutes." It was the Paws 'N' Claws volunteer again. This time her hands were in her hair, the leash stretched tight down to her dog's harness. He craned his neck around to look up at her. "We have ten minutes before the Waddle starts. WHERE'S OUR HOUND DAWG?"

"I will run!" Aneta bent to tighten a loose lace on the right foot.

Vee's phone rang. Aneta froze, crouched. Sunny and Esther clutched each other. Now everyone would believe them. Mr. Leonard would not run a puppy mill anymore in Oakton. C.P. looked from one to another, shrugged, and pulled an apple from a leg pocket of his cargo pants. He crunched while he watched.

Vee whipped the phone out of her back pocket and punched the green button. Sunny and Esther crowded close. The Paws 'N' Claws volunteer darted off, muttering about children and cell phones and what was the world coming to. Aneta didn't dare move.

"Yes," Vee said. Aneta shot a look toward the Leonards' house. The brown truck was gone. Nadine's Toyota left Mr. Leonard's street and turned away from The Sweet Stuff to park where there was still some street-side parking.

"Oh," Vee said, her dark brows pulling together. "Okay." She punched off the phone and stuck it back in her pocket. Her brows lifted, and she raised her shoulders. "They didn't find any puppies."

"How could they not find puppies?" Sunny stamped her foot. "All the clues were there!"

Aneta rose to her feet. The tears drizzled down her cheeks, but she brushed them away. They could not do anything more about Mr. Leonard. They needed the Hound Dawg. She would find a Hound Dawg. She took off running through the gathering crowd, looking for Zeff. When she reached the middle of the park, she stopped, panting, and slowly turned in a circle. No Cousin Zeff. Now what?

She heard her name. Her gaze caught waving arms back at The Sweet Stuff parking lot. She squinted. The girls, waving and pointing past her. She turned. There, at the end of the park, nearing the path down to the lake was the Hound Dawg! Who had the girls gotten to wear it? Almost too tall for the suit itself. *Whatever.* The girls had come through.

She relaxed. She would thank the kind person. In August, the Hound Dawg would soon be a *hot* dog with the morning air warming quickly. Before she could move, however, something smacked her arm, and she cried out, wheeling. C.P. stood next to her, hands on his bent knees, breathing hard.

"Wink—!" he got out.

Alarm crackled out the tips of her fingers. No puppy at the end of the leash. "Where's Wink?"

Chapter 21

Who's Got Wink?

$\mathcal{S}$ome giant, furry paw bashed me in the head." C.P., trying not to cry, gazed wildly about the crowd.

A big, hairy paw? Had C.P. had too much fried dough? What was he talking about? She told herself to calm down. She thought of two Squad members. What did Sunny and Esther do when things went wrong? When Esther muttered, she was usually praying, Aneta had learned. Sunny would talk to God as if He were standing with them. God standing with her sounded good right now.

"Okay, Sunny's God," Aneta said under her breath. "Someone takes Wink. Please help me find him safe."

"Aneta! Aneeee–TAH!" Both C.P. and Aneta turned toward the sound. Vee, with long legs that ate up the grass of the park, hair falling out of her ponytail. She was pointing past them. C.P. and Aneta turned.

At the edge of the park, walking down the road toward the lake, was the Hound Dawg. What was he or she doing there? The Waddle was beginning any minute.

"Wink! Wink!" Aneta called, peering at the bassets thronging toward The Sweet Stuff. Too many long ears on tricolored small bodies among big dog bodies. Tears burned out of her eyes. "Oh, Wink!" she screamed.

When Vee blew past her, still pointing, Aneta heard her shout, "The Hound—Wink!" Without understanding—only hearing "Wink!"—Aneta charged after her friend. She yelled at C.P., "Get my mom! Get the police!" He veered off and headed into the crowd. Ahead, a kid and its mother approached the Hound. The mom lifted the child up toward the Hound's arms. The costumed figure jerked away.

Then she saw it in the Hound's furry arms.

A small, tricolored basset with a red harness!

"Stop!" Vee yelled. With a quick look toward them, the Hound broke into a dead run toward the lake. Aneta ducked past this person and that group, slowed at every move. All the people who would donate to Paws 'N' Claws Animal Buddies, all the probable Waddle watchers were getting in the way. When she shouted, "Help! Help! Stop that Hound!" people chuckled and clapped. *They think it's part of the Waddle!*

The Waddle. Wink and his secret costume and a forever home. The air horn blast split the morning air. Cheers broke out; the crowds jostled her to get a good viewing spot. She pushed through, jumping up to keep an eye on Vee and the Hound. She smacked into the broad back of a large man bending to give cotton candy to a small boy. Knocked flat and breathless, she gasped, "Please, God, keep Wink safe."

She staggered to her feet. The gargantuan Jasper breakfast reconsidered its location. For a few moments, she couldn't run, couldn't think. *Wink!* Her legs kicked into gear like they did after she dove into the pool. *Faster, Aneta, faster.*

She could see Vee's white shirt disappearing around the bend. The Hound was already out of sight. What if the Hound did something to Vee? Who was this Hound, and why did he kidnap her little Wink?

She rounded the corner, pounding down the path to the lake. Two figures were struggling on the dock.

Chapter 22

The Race

*A*neta shrieked in terror. The Hound, costume stretched up the too-tall frame, dangled Wink over the water while he twisted Vee's arm behind her.

Vee screamed and bent forward. As the Hound leaned with her, Vee whipped her head up and bashed the Hound in the chin. Hard. He dropped her arm, but before she could run, he bellowed in pain and shoved her off the dock. Wink began to howl.

"Vee! Stop! Oh, Vee!" Aneta ran on.

Vee cried out once before she smacked the water like a rag doll. The Hound, with the yelping Wink under one arm, untied the boat. He stepped in and dumped Wink on the floor of the boat. Grabbing the oars, he rowed out into the lake.

Aneta pelted down the dock. "Vee!"

Vee stood, wiped lake water from her eyes, and held the top of her head. She began to slog to shore. "That Hound has a hard head." She waved Aneta away. "I'm fine! Go save Wink! I'm running for help!" Squishing water and mud, she darted up the hill.

Aneta hoped C.P. had *already* found help. Past getting to

Wink, she didn't know *what* she was going to do. It appeared the Hound would stop at nothing to carry off Wink. But why?

Leaping into the next rowboat, she squatted to regain her balance then pushed at the dock. The end of the boat floated away from the dock. She pushed again. "C'mon, stupid boat!" Her glance fell on the rope at the bow. Still tied to the dock. "Oh, please, please, please!" Tears made it difficult to see the rope. She frantically glanced over her shoulder. The Hound dipped the oars, pulling farther from her, a V-line widening from the bow. A little smooth head popped up on the seat. Then one paw. Wink would never be able to balance if he made it up on the rocking seat.

"Wink!" she called. "Stay!" Did he know stay? After what seemed like forever, she scrabbled the knot off the metal cleat. Terrible moments of futile splashing followed. Finally she settled into a dip-pull, dip-pull that sent the heavy, wooden rowboat gliding across a glassy lake.

Oh, Wink, Wink. She strained to see over her shoulder. Had she gained on the boat? Handicapped by the big furry paws that had smacked C.P., the Hound frequently lost its grip on the oars. Aneta's steady dip-pull, dip-pull was shortening the distance. Now she could hear muffled shouts from the immense stuffed head. Wink put a second paw on the seat. He raised his head like a prairie dog peering out of its hole.

"Stay, boy!" She pulled harder. Pain shot up into her shoulders. Who *was* that Hound? Some crazy Waddle walker who wanted to make sure Wink was out of the running for the costume contest?

On shore, two police cars—sirens shrieking—and Nadine's Toyota skidded at the end of the gravel road. Frank and Nadine leaped out. The police officers dashed for the remaining rowboats.

Then Aneta saw Mom. Sprinting in her sandals, she staggered a bit in the sand, but never took her eyes off Aneta's boat.

"I'm coming, sweetie!" she yelled. Her long blond hair fell out of the ponytail and streamed behind her. She landed on the dock first and leaped into a boat. Frank, moving faster than Aneta had ever seen him move, thudded into the boat after Mom. Nadine gestured and stayed on the dock. Before Frank sat down, Mom was rowing.

"Mom! Mom!" A quick look over her shoulder told her she was nearly to the Hound's boat. His shouting sounded meaner and meaner. The two police officers, a man and a short, stocky woman, jumped into the next boat and rowed after Mom and Frank.

Up on the road cascaded a stream of brightly colored scooters, skidding on the gravel. The Fam. But not to the rescue. They could not help her now. It was all up to her.

Another look. The Hound had stopped rowing. Standing awkwardly in the boat, he lurched back and forth. Wink had disappeared, although she could still hear him yipping. He must have fallen back under the seat. Good. He was safer there. At least for the moment. What did the Hound have planned for her little Wink?

The Hound staggered. The boat tipped sharply. A long ear flipped up from the bottom of the boat and then disappeared. Aneta screamed, pulling harder on the oars. The Hound steadied himself, looked up at her, yelled something she couldn't make out, and swatted the air. He slipped and crashed to his knees. More stifled sounds.

With two last mighty dip-pulls that made her shoulders scream, Aneta bumped the other boat. Grabbing its side, she yelled, "Stop!" Still on his knees, reaching under the seat, the Hound turned its furry head toward her. Where was Wink? Ignoring the arm warning her away, she peered into the boat. No sight of a long tricolored body. "Wink!" she shouted. "Here, Wink!"

"Get away!" the Hound hollered. These words she understood. "Troublemaker!" That word was clear, too. With one arm on the gunwale for balance, the Hound rose and steadied himself, towering over Aneta. Remembering what he'd done to Vee, a shiver of fear chased through her. What was he going to do to *her*? Stomp on her hand to make her let go? She clutched the side more tightly. A splinter poked into her thumb. Staring up at him, he was a monster clown hound a thousand feet high.

"Give me Wink!" she yelled, leaning farther out of her boat to look in the Hound's boat. Sure enough, there was Wink, semistanding and tumbling on his side as he stumbled toward her. He tripped on one of his ears and took a nosedive. He cried. Aneta's heart wrenched.

The Hound steadied himself and pulled an oar out of the oarlock. He raised it to shoulder height. Horror rocked Aneta. Was he going to bean her on the head?

Chapter 23

Who *Is* That Hound?

The Hound punched Aneta's boat with the oar, setting off waves that bounced both boats. "Get—ah—here!" she heard. Her arms felt like they would rip from her shoulders as the boat pitched. *I will not. Let. Go.*

To her right, she saw the two rowboats pushing through the water. Mom was pulling hard while she looked over her shoulder at the drama behind her. "You touch my daughter, and I will make sure you *never* see daylight again!" Help would be there in seconds. Could she hold on? Pain streaked down her arms.

The Hound landed another mighty thud to Aneta's boat. The oar hit the water. So did the Hound with a very human scream. The big head sank.

Aneta caught her breath, letting go of the boat. The big head resurfaced; the Hound thrashed the water, fighting to remove the cumbersome head. As the boat floated away, Aneta saw Wink hanging halfway over the side of the boat!

"No, Wink!" she shrieked, stretching out her hand. The white tippy tail swung in a happy circle. "Stay! Stay, boy!" Save the

Hound? Save Wink? She threw herself between the two boats, and with fire erupting in all her muscles, clawed the Hound's boat toward her. More splinters stung. In another moment, she had lunged forward enough to grab Wink by the scruff of his neck and pull him to safety in her boat. With him on the floor, she took the oar closest to the Hound and dipped it into the water, swinging the boat nearer to him. "Grab the oar! Hold on to it!"

The Hound swatted away the oar and sank again.

"Take it!" she screamed.

Wink howled.

"It's okay, Aneta. Sit down; we've got him," came a firm voice next to her. The female police officer maneuvered their boat next to the thrashing Hound. The two officers hauled the sodden Hound into the boat and removed the head.

Aneta sucked in a breath. *Mr. Leonard?*

"Troublemaker!" he yelled between coughing and choking.

After shipping the oar to the side of the boat, Aneta collapsed on the bottom next to Wink. Trembling, she pulled the puppy into her lap. She leaned over him, murmuring, "Thank You, God" over and over. Her shoulders jerked uncontrollably.

The boat rocked, and then Mom was there. "Oh, sweetie." She gathered Aneta and Wink in her arms, holding them so tightly Wink whimpered. Aneta looked up. Pushing the words out, she said, "You're pushing the peanut-butter jar into my rib cage, sweetie."

Mom burst into tears. So did Aneta.

Chapter 24

Crocs Killer!

Vee and The Fam met them at the shore, pulling the boat way up. Mom helped Aneta out; she hugged Wink and clung to her mother. Her Mom. Her Fam. Her friends.

"You're a hero, Aneta," Vee said, her eyes round with awe. "That was amazing." She clutched Aneta's hand. Aneta cried out.

"Let me see your hands," her mother demanded. She inspected the slivers and pulled most of them out. Aneta dug out the last one.

Vee darted forward and hugged her quickly, leaving water patches on Aneta's T-shirt and shorts.

"Is your head okay?" Aneta asked, returning the hug.

"My stepdad says it's a good thing I have a hard head." She smiled the biggest smile Aneta had seen her smile. Beyond her, Aneta saw all the parents talking as Mr. Leonard was led away to the police cars. Siblings stood wide-eyed and pointing at Mr. Leonard. "He's proud of me. He said I run like an Olympian." Vee's wet hair clung to her glowing face.

C.P. stepped forward, a half-eaten corn dog in his hand.

Chewing, he offered the rest to Aneta. "You need food? That was a lot of work."

"Aneeeeetah!" It was Esther's high, nasal voice.

Aneta turned to see Esther and Sunny trotting down the gravel. Esther waved her arms. "C'mon! The Waddle!"

Sunny yelled, "We can still make it! Those bassets waddle reeeeealllllly slow!"

Esther towed the covered wagon. Sunny wore Aneta's messenger bag slung across her chest. She patted it and said in a false whisper, "I've got the secret weapon!"

Turning to Mom, Aneta grinned. Mom threw up her hands. "More surprises? Well, I guess being your mom will be a life of surprises." She ruffled her daughter's hair. "I'm good with that." She gave her a little push. "Go. I'll be there, Aneta Jasper. Always."

"The Waddle is just turning the corner to go past the community center. We can meet them there." Esther headed up the hill with the wagon. Sunny handed the bag to Aneta while Vee's dad handed his daughter the clipboard she'd dropped on her sprint after the Hound.

Loud voices, the two officers and an unfamiliar one, split the air as the rest of the group turned to head up the hill. A woman pushed between Sunny's parents, planting herself in front of Aneta and Wink.

Startled, Aneta drew Wink to her chest and involuntarily stepped back. She sensed Mom behind her.

"You troublemakers!" the woman growled, stamping her foot like a two-year-old.

"What?" Aneta stammered. She tried to go around. The woman stepped in front of her, preventing her passage.

"Excuse me," Mom said, stepping to Aneta's side. "Who are you?"

But Aneta knew. It was *her*.

Taking in the angry eyes under a khaki Puppy Pellets cap, Aneta's gaze traveled down past dark shorts to the woman's feet. Her eyes widened.

Beige Crocs with a high line of mud.

"The Crocs Killer!" Vee, Esther, and Sunny's voices blended in a discordant screech from halfway up the hill.

Stepping up close—way too close—the woman's face furrowed in angry lines. A deep tan cracked her face into many wrinkles. Aneta was pretty sure none of them were the result of smiling. "You sicced animal control on us," she said, leaning close to Aneta. "Nosy kids." Then she grimaced. "And they found nothing, did they?"

Us?

Aneta looked at the Squad who had come back down the hill. Mr. Leonard had a wife!

Mom, with her arm around Aneta, moved to pass the woman. The woman, however, stepped in front of Mom so quickly that Mom bumped into her.

"Oh, so you want to get in my face?" Mrs. Leonard pushed at Mom. Aneta thought for sure Mom would move away, but she did the opposite. She took a step closer to the woman so they were nose to nose. Uh-oh. Mom was going to do a Jasper-ish thing.

Chapter 25

Who Will Win?

Leave my mother alone!" Aneta forced herself between the two women. Wink yelped. "You are a bad person, trying to kill Wink."

Wink's wriggling caught Mrs. Leonard's eye. "That dog has been nothing but problems since he was born. Freak—with that bad eye. He's no worth to anyone."

Aneta gasped. *How could she say that?*

The male police officer stepped up and placed a hand on Mrs. Leonard, who continued to shout. Mom regained what Aneta called her "lawyer face," maneuvering Aneta past the spluttering woman and up the hill toward the girls. "Thanks, 'Neta. That woman wanted a fight, and unfortunately, I wanted to give her one. Thanks, sweetie, too, for saying 'my mother.' Do you know that's the first time you've called me that?"

"You are such a Jasper, Mom," Aneta said with a shaky smile.

"So are you, sweetie."

"You got everything?" Sunny was twirling with her head tilted back. The girls were in front of the community center, waiting for the tail end of the Waddle to waddle past.

"Time for the reveal," Esther said with a grin, whipping off the cover to the wagon.

"Wow." Vee admired a miniature, real-looking desk. "You and your sibs did a great job. What's it made out of?"

Esther pointed. "Cardboard, except for where Wink sits. The seat is my little brother's square stool to reach the sink in the bathroom. He wanted Wink to sit on it."

Sunny joined them. "Where's the sign?"

Esther drew it out from under the desk. The girls read it in unison and broke up laughing. "Good enough?"

"More than!" Aneta said, her eyes crinkling. "Oh, Esther. This will work."

They slid a squirmy Wink into his costume. He aroo'd a few times in protest. Aneta hung the last prop over the collar of her T-shirt for later and held him in the crook of her arm.

"Ready, action!" Sunny sang out, spinning around the group. The tail end of the parade waddled by. Esther pulled the wagon into position. Wink whined and tried to wriggle out of Aneta's arms to join the final three bassets padding along. Two of them had white tip-top tails circling the air like Wink, while the third carried his like a question mark.

Aneta knelt and kissed Wink on the top of his velvety head, whispering, "Okay, here we go." She wanted to ask God again for Wink, but with the help given for battling the Hound, she thought maybe she shouldn't bug Him too much. She set Wink on his perch and nodded to Esther, who pulled on the handle of the wagon. They were off. The last hope for Wink and his forever home as a Jasper.

"A basset is an asset! And we have a fine bunch of bassets with bassetude today for Oakton's first Basset Waddle. Judging by the pledge sheets that have been turned in and tallied, we will definitely do this again next year!" The mayor cleared his throat then announced the top three Waddlers who'd gathered the most pledges for Paws 'N' Claws Animal Buddies. Each received a stuffed basset hound as a prize.

"Now," he continued. "On to the judging for the King and Queen of the Waddle! Contestants, please slowly walk your dogs before the judges on the reviewing stand."

While he gave instructions, Aneta stood on her tiptoes, looking over the other people holding leashes or pulling carts and wagons. Where was her mother? She smiled. *Her mother.* Finally, she felt like Mom was *her* mother. Looking back and forth at the growing crowd standing below the elevated judges' platform, she located her mother standing with the rest of The Fam. Her mom was waving.

The head judge finished with, "When you get to the stand, turn and face your dog in the judges' direction so we can get a really good look at your dog and the costume. Then head to The Sweet Stuff parking lot for a treat for you and your Waddler!"

Aneta placed the final piece of costume on Wink's long nose. He shook it off.

"Just wait until we stand in front of the judges and put them on then," Vee suggested.

A few more pulls with the wagon, and Wink was before the judges. Vee, Sunny, and Esther stood apart so the judges would get a good look at Wink in his costume.

"Last and certainly not least, we have Wink, who is available for adoption through Paws 'N' Claws Animal Buddies—"

Aneta's smile froze as she slipped the dark-rimmed glasses on Wink. This time he didn't shake them off, only tilted his long nose up at her. And winked. A sob leaped out of her throat. The judge's voice was sprightly and cheerful. Like he was saying a good thing and not breaking Aneta's heart. She had always known Wink was adoptable. It was just—just—

The judge continued. "The adoption booth of Paws 'N' Claws Animal Buddies is taking applications for adoption for Wink and many other dogs."

Laughter swelled as the crowd noticed Wink's little suit and tie along with the glasses, seated behind a desk that looked like a courtroom desk.

"According to the card here, it appears that Wink is dressed as Mr. B. H. Barker, Esquire, Attorney at Paw! Complete with spectacles!" Applause fluttered and grew in the midmorning air. Aneta carefully watched Mom. She was wiping her eyes. A good sign? The Fam was laughing. No surprise there. Aneta forced the smile to stay on her face. How many people would rush to adopt her Wink? Oh dear. Her legs had stopped working.

"Our turn's over. Start walking, Aneta." Vee's calm voice pulled Aneta from her jumbled thoughts.

Dogs and people milled in front of the judges' stand during the deliberations. Soon, the sound system squealed. The Squad held hands and Wink's leash. The glasses were once again tucked over the collar of Aneta's shirt.

"Residents of fair Oakton! We have our King and Queen of the first annual Oakton Founders' Day Basset Waddle." He held up a piece of paper with a flourish and read: "Queen of the Waddle is Elder Clara, the resident drooler at the Oakton Residence for Seniors. Dressed as Little Red Riding Hood's grandmother!"

Please oh please, let Wink win. She remembered the last time she'd said, "Please oh please." She'd been dreading winning a poster contest. Dreading having to speak in front of people. Dreading working with girls she didn't know. Look how it had all turned out! She'd spoken in front of a large group twice and hadn't died. The girls were now her best friends. Wink, however, still did not have a forever home with Aneta.

". . .For Mr. B. H. Barker, Esquire, Attorney at Paw!" She hadn't been paying attention. Squeals erupted from the other Squadders. She was encased in a group hug, including Wink. Louder shrieks as they tipped over into a big pile on the ground. Wink, safe inside Aneta's arms, slurped up the side of her face.

"See?" Sunny untangled herself, giggling. "He's proud to be King!"

The Queen and King of the Waddle were placed on a mini stage. Nadine placed the crowns on their heads. Elder Clara promptly lay down and showed her belly for rubs. Wink stomped on his ears, sat back, and aroo-aroo'd. The crowd shouted with laughter. The girls giggled. The Waddle was a success. Wink was King!

Chapter 26

Not *More* Trouble?

$\mathcal{A}$ warm breeze swept across the park, and basset noses lifted to read the air. In a flash, Wink had tumbled off the low platform onto the grass, righted himself, and hurtled across the park toward the vendor booths on the opposite side. Not once did he stumble on his ears. Sometimes it appeared that all four feet were off the ground at once!

"Where's he going?" Sunny yelled, chasing after him and being unsuccessful.

"Could be *anywhere*! Too many smells!" panted Esther, pulling up the rear and puffing mightily.

"He's stopped at that van behind the Puppy Pellets booth." Vee stopped so abruptly, Aneta collided with her. "Ouch. Sorry. But that's *the* van! My clipboard says the Leonards have the Puppy Pellets booth. That white van from the park last night was *their* van!"

Wink's nose skimmed the ground. He ran up to the back door of the long, panel-work van parked at a right angle between the tables and began to bay, "Aroo! Aroo!"

Faint answering bays came from the inside!

"The evidence!" Esther ran to the door and pulled on it. Locked. "It must be those dogs from Mr. Leonard's garage. How long have they been in there? We've got to get them out." She looked around wildly. Aneta thought if her friend had a stick she would have smashed the window. "Mr. and Mrs. Leonard have the key! It's too hot. They'll die!" Esther began to cry, continuing to tug on the door.

Sunny spun around to face the girls, her face alive with determination. "I know how we save those dogs *and* get our evidence." She took off back across the field, waving her arms and jumping as though it was all part of the show.

"The King and his nose!" she yelled as she approached the judges' stand. "The King has detected a surprise with his powerful nose!"

The mayor leaned over and handed her the microphone. "Well, nobody told me about this stunt, but it sounds like fun. Go ahead, Sunny."

Sunny took the mic and backed up with large dramatic steps, all the while keeping her eyes on the crowd and talking. "Ladies and gentlemen! The King has found a secret scent. It must be in that van. Shall we open it and see?"

Aneta stood, keeping an eye on Wink. She heard her friend's voice boom over the microphone. What was she up to? Those had to be the poor dogs from the Leonards' garage. But how to get the van open? The day had become so hot, Aneta wished she'd worn a hat. How long could they survive in the heat of a closed van?

The crowd, appearing to embrace another Waddle event to coordinate with the Hound Dawg chase, the city band, the Blessing of the Hounds, and the crowning of costumed royalty, began to chant. "Open, open, open!"

From across the park, Aneta saw Sunny wave at the animal control officer who had checked the Leonards' garage that morning. He looked puzzled at her wild gesturing but joined her. Holding the mic away from her, she whispered to him. He straightened and ran toward his truck. Sunny began to bounce up and down. "Well, folks, we have a brave volunteer to open the door."

By now, other bassets were joining Wink in the howling. Once ten did, fifteen more began to howl. Shivers shot up Aneta's spine. The chorus grew louder and more eerie. Several dogs broke loose from owners too caught up in the show to hold tight to leashes and began to run around the park. The noise level streaked upward until Sunny had to shout above the crowd and the hounds. "Hang on, folks!"

The officer returned with a thin piece of metal. He crossed the park and went up to the van.

"What's that?" Aneta asked, pointing to the metal.

"Called a 'slim jim,'" he replied, sliding the thin strip of metal down into the driver's-side window. The lock popped open.

"It is open!" roared Sunny into the mic.

"Hooray!" the crowd yelled and clapped.

Once the officer had unlocked the front door, he disappeared into the van. The crowd quieted expectantly until the back doors burst open. Aneta scooped up Wink to get him out of the way. A wave of heat gushed from the van.

The crowd roared, "Opened! Opened—" then fell abruptly silent.

Inside the van, stacked in crates two high and four across, were basset hound puppies and several adult dogs. Not all of them were howling. Some were not moving.

Chapter 27

Things Change

$\mathcal{A}$while later, Mr. Martin reached for another chip on his plate. "Good thing Wink had that basset nose." He and his wife sat together in the park pavilion along with the Squadder parents and the girls. Brothers and sisters played nearby on the playground, loudly disputing who had rights to the top of the slide. "Those dogs in the van would have never made it."

"Nadine was able to resuscitate the two who were unconscious. I think the vet will keep them all overnight for observation. One of the techs is going to stay with them." Frank put an affectionate arm around his wife. "She's handy to have around." He turned to the S.A.V.E. Squad who were sitting together, finishing up grilled chicken, fresh fruit, and Gram's baba ghanoush and pita chips. "Remember your first meeting? I thought for sure Esther and Vee would kill each other, Aneta would quit, and Sunny would never settle down. Boy, was I wrong!" He dipped his head. "Good job, girls. You taught me not to judge by first appearances."

The girls giggled.

"We were brats," Sunny admitted. "But now we're the S.A.V.E. Squad." She linked arms with Aneta on one side, Esther on the other. Esther linked with Vee. Vee smiled her smile. Aneta wondered if the other girls were thinking the same thing she was—the longer the adults talked, the longer the girls would get to be together before they were banished.

"How did you girls put it all together?" Mrs. Nguyen leaned against her husband as he dug into his second piece of apple pie.

Aneta looked between the two couples who were Vee's parents. One set sat at the far end of the table. The other across from her and the girls. What would it be like to have four parents? Did everybody like each other? Other than twice—today and when she admitted she feared being sent away—Vee did not talk about her family. Ever. Like she also never said where she went with the backpack.

"It was Aneta." Esther leaned forward, pointing at her friend with a fork full of macaroni salad. "Aneta remembered Mrs. Leonard—the Crocs Killer—wore a Puppy Pellet hat. And we found out at the Pets Emporium that you can only get a Puppy Pellet hat if you buy lots of Puppy Pellets."

"Was the owner of the Pets Emporium buying Mr. Leonard's puppies?" Esther's father asked, spearing a pickle off his wife's plate. She glared at him then laughed.

"Yes," Vee replied. "Some of those puppies were sick, too. Animal control is talking to him."

"I don't think he'll be buying puppies again." Sunny scooped up the last glob of baba ghanoush from her paper plate with a pita chip.

"Nadine is going to talk with him about working with Paws 'N' Claws to showcase dogs who need homes instead," Frank said.

"I'll help convince him." Gram smiled.

The girls laughed.

"And all because of Aneta," Mom said, her brilliant smile flashing.

"Aneta is brilliant," Sunny added.

A silence fell as people returned to their food. Esther's voice broke the crunching and chewing.

"If I hadn't won that contest, I would never have gotten in the S.A.V.E. Squad," Esther remarked, staring at her plate. Her voice was so low, the entire table quieted to listen. "These girls are nice. Not all girls are."

A pause.

"Yeah, and we're stupid. Together." Sunny made everyone laugh.

Her parents stood up. "And that brings us to the banishment."

Esther elbowed Sunny and hissed in her ear, "You weren't supposed to bring that up. Now we all have to go home and never see each other again."

Aneta was thinking the same thing.

Sunny reddened. She set her spoon down.

"I have a suggestion," Mr. Quinlan said, glancing around at the other parents. "Perhaps we could suspend the banishment. Think of something else to help them remember wisdom?"

Mom's face brightened. "Perhaps our families could get together now and then until school starts." Glancing up and down the long tables, she raised her brows. "What do you think? The girls can be together under supervision. We could do Pool Plashes at our house." She flushed. "If you want to, that is."

Aneta remembered the embarrassment she'd dumped on her mom. *Never again.*

Vee's sets of parents turned to themselves and murmured. So did the Martins. After a few moments, all turned back to Mr. Quinlan.

"Agreed." Vee's two sets nodded.

"Agreed." Sunny's parents smiled.

"Agreed." Esther's parents looked pleased.

Sunny leaped off the bench and began to twirl. "Oh, yayness!" she yelled.

The other three jumped up, grabbed Sunny, and began to hop up and down.

"The S.A.V.E. Squad is still together!" Vee said with a grin.

Aneta thought her heart would burst. No banishment. Five weeks remained of summer vacation. Now it would be filled with the S.A.V.E. Squad, scooters, and fun. Only one thing would make her happier. She glanced at her mother, who tipped her head toward the dessert booth kitty-corner from their pavilion. "Dessert?" she mouthed.

Aneta gave her a thumbs-up and excused herself from the girls. "Dessert and my mom," she explained.

Walking arm in arm, after a silence that wrapped Aneta like a soft blanket, Mom spoke.

"I've been thinking, Aneta." Mom matched her slightly longer stride to Aneta's. "Maybe you and I are ready for a basset in our family."

"Maybe means yes! Oh! Oh!" was all Aneta could say. She straightened herself and hugged her mom sideways. She turned her mom toward her. She made her face very serious and said with careful English, "Okay, Mom, have you considered the responsibilities of pet ownership?"

Mom smothered a chuckle then put on an equally serious

face. They resumed their walk. "I have. Like pets need fresh water at all times. But I work all day." She slanted a glance at Aneta.

Aneta jumped in. "I will be the water checker. I know where to get a dog waterer that holds two gallons. As Wink drinks, the water comes out."

Mom was smiling. "Now, bassets are hounds and—"

"Hounds bark," Aneta supplied. She looked worried. "Nadine won't let someone adopt one of their dogs if they're going to leave it outside." She stopped walking. "What about the pool?"

Mom nodded, gently pulling her along. "I've talked to Nadine a lot about this. Our dog *will* be an inside dog. I'll get the pool fenced."

"What about the cleanup?" Aneta wanted to know. She thought about how the owner of the Pets Emporium said people didn't want to see dog doo-doo. She hoped Mom knew that dogs did that. They were nearly at the dessert tent.

"I was hoping a certain girl I know would be the master of that."

"I know that girl!" Aneta gave a hop of happiness. Was she dreaming? This was better than having Mom just say yes. They were having a *Jasper discussion*!

"And are we talking about a certain basset that needs to join our forever home?" Mom asked as they waited their turn for the sweet treats.

"Yes, oh yes! Little Wink!" Aneta drew in a deep breath. Mother and daughter suspended their Jasper discussion and turned their attention to homemade cheesecakes, brownies, and a chilly root-beer float, finally selecting a wedge of cherry cheesecake to share.

Instead of meandering back to the pavilion to join the others, however, Mom steered Aneta toward a booth four booths down. They passed the face-painting booth, cotton-candy booth, and the food-drive booth with an unhappy Melissa sitting behind a table with bags of canned goods in front of her. She pretended not to see them. That was okay with Aneta.

Then she saw where she hoped, hoped, *hoped* Mom would stop. The closer they got, the faster Aneta's heart beat. Stepping under the awning, they approached a man sitting at the table.

Mom nudged her. "Tell the man what you'd like."

"We would like to apply to adopt Wink," Aneta said, cherishing each word. Her forever pet in her forever life. While the man shuffled through a list labeled ADOPTABLES, she lifted a forkful of cherry cheesecake into her mouth. The sweet, rich flavor rushed over her tongue. Today was truly a perfect day.

"Is that the petite basset with the squint? The King of the Waddle?"

"Yes, Wink."

"That sure was a clever costume."

"That's my daughter," Mom said with a nudge into Aneta's ribs. "She's very creative."

"Wink, you say?" He was looking down at a paper. "Oh."

"I kind of named him when I rescued him." A shiver of happiness spiraled up Aneta's spine.

"Oh, you're the one." He looked like he might cry, she thought. Why did the man look sad? This was a happy day. If she were Sunny, she would be twirling.

"I'm sorry," the man said. "He's off the adoptable list."

The cheesecake tasted like dirt. Mom's arm encircled her waist.

"Could—could—" Mom's voice faltered. "Could we be a

backup application? Sometimes things fall through."

The man shook his head. "I'm sorry." He gestured to the paper. "There are five backup applications on Wink."

This sweet day had turned terribly sour.

Chapter 28

Forever Homes

It was a cool evening for late August. The sun had long gone down; the flaming tiki torches surrounding the patio reflected in the occasional rippling of the pool. White twinkle lights hung from the fence top. Walking through the doorway with the fourth basket of Gram's homemade tortilla chips to go with the bowls of Jasper guacamole and sour cream mixed with salsa, Aneta watched the Nguyens chatting with the Martins. Mom, Gram, and the Quinlans were having a lively discussion on immigration issues. Just what a Jasper loved—discussion! Vee's other set were listening in, adding bits here and there. *No younger siblings tonight, just the older kids,* Aneta thought with satisfaction. And, of course, C.P.

As she set down the basket, C.P. rose up from sitting with his feet in the pool. He closed the gate to the pool and inspected the tray.

"No more peanut-butter cookies?" he asked, turning his mouth down.

Aneta snorted. "Sorry. We are now out of peanut-butter cookies."

"Oh well, I'll suffer," he said, grabbing a chip and dipping into the green dip.

Turning away, she walked over to the three girls threading beads onto leather cords at the patio table. The S.A.V.E. Squad. Tonight the parents had surprised them by telling them sleepovers could start again.

"Although," Sunny's mother said, looking at Mom, "let's keep getting together. I've really been enjoying our gatherings."

Mom nodded vigorously.

"Here—here's your leather cord. Esther's got a different color for each Squadder. My bead is red-and-white spirals for my hair and twirling," Sunny instructed, using one finger to push the bead toward Aneta. "This multicolored one is for Esther and all the colors she paints her nails." That bead rolled next to the spiral-striped one.

Esther beamed, displaying two hands with a different color on each nail. Aneta sat down and threaded them on a leather string. "What's Vee's color?" Aneta asked, tying a knot after each bead to keep them from sliding. She liked the idea of Squad bracelets. It made them, well, more Squad-y.

"A long, skinny bead." Vee laughed. She stuck out her legs. "For all that running I did!"

Everyone laughed. Aneta scanned the table. "I don't see my bead."

"That's because your mom had a special one made." Sunny motioned to Aneta's mother.

Mom stood up and took a jewelry box from her pocket. Aneta looked questioningly at her mother when she handed her the box. Opening it quickly, Aneta saw a bead the color of pool water lying on the cotton. Two words in cursive were engraved in the flat, oval bead. *Aneta Jasper*. She turned it over. *S.A.V.E. Squad*.

"Mom!" she said and took out the bead.

"Yes," her mother said. "It's official. Your first name has been legally changed back to Aneta. But you're still a Jasper."

The girls looked very pleased. "We were in on it," Sunny said. "We all have one with our names and S.A.V.E. Squad."

Aneta gazed at the bead with *Aneta Jasper* on it. She sighed and then threw her arms around her mother's waist.

"I did not think the summer would turn out this way," she said, rejoining the girls a few moments later.

"Saving dogs wasn't even on my list of things to do during the summer!" Vee said, a corner of her mouth turned up. She slanted a look at Esther, who made a face.

"Your lists! I guess they saved us for the Waddle, though." Esther lifted one of her fingers to inspect a chip in the polish.

"But Wink—" Aneta stopped. So much had happened. Her mom had said she had learned a lot. Some of it hurt. How could people treat animals that way? A deep sigh welled up within her at the same time as a long pink tongue slurped her ankle. She grinned and bent down.

The not-so-small-anymore, tricolored puppy wriggled and tried to do the same to her face. She nuzzled his neck. She'd washed him today; he smelled like lavender. Her Wink. As she set him down, he hop-stomped over to a larger dog with the same markings, leaning against Gram's leg. The older female nudged him with her nose, licking under his ears. Wink closed his eyes in doggy delight.

"It is so funny that all the people on the waiting list for Wink were your relatives!" Esther said.

Mom answered. "Aneta's grandmother started it. Then the rest of The Fam added their names in case she didn't clear adoption. They were going to make sure Wink got his forever home with a Jasper if I didn't change my mind."

"And then your grandmother adopts Wink's mother. At least we *think* Baba is his mother," Vee said, sliding a striped bead onto her cord. "She looks more like him than your Uncle Luke's Ethel." She set down her bracelet to face Aneta. "Is Ethel better now?"

Gram answered her from nearby. "Oh yes. Luke has her out walking every day. She's getting better food than Puppy Pellets, and her coat is shiny. You'll see her one of these days. Luke's got a basket for her on his scooter."

"Nadine is working on adopting the other puppies out," Mom said, stretching her legs out in front of her. "Paws 'N' Claws Animal Buddies does good work finding forever homes."

"Good," Sunny said with a bounce of her head.

"Well," Zeff said, standing and stretching from his spot by C.P. "I gotta head. Early courier route tomorrow." He helped a medium-sized, tricolored basset up to a standing position. The dog staggered a moment then shook himself. "Me and the Fred gotta get."

"How are his back legs coming?" Mrs. Martin asked, dipping a pita chip into the guacamole.

"I massage his legs." Zeff looked down at the dog who gazed up at him, long snout quivering, eyes drooping. "He might always limp, but he's definitely better." He slowly led the older dog toward the french doors.

"Sunny, did you tell the girls about your new dog?" Mrs. Quinlan asked with a grin.

Vee, Esther, and Aneta whipped their heads around to glare at Sunny, who was giving her mother the "shh" look with a finger to her lips.

"Mom! I wanted to surprise them by inviting them to the house to see her."

"Her?"

"What is she?"

"How could you not tell us?"

"I thought your brothers had asthma?" The questions came fast and furious.

Sunny pulled a picture from her pocket. "You can see her right here." She passed it around. Aneta saw a gigantic dog sitting in a desert scene.

"Where did you take this? It is not around here," she said, passing it on to Vee, who inspected it closely before passing it on to Esther.

"C'mon, Sunny, don't keep them in suspense," her dad said, standing up. "You're being a tease."

Sunny burst into giggles. "All right," she said, collecting her picture and gazing at it fondly before returning it to her pocket. "Her name is Dezzie. She's a giant mixed breed—"

"We could *see* that," Vee muttered.

"She's our cyber dog," Sunny continued, ignoring Vee. "We adopted her from Big Dog Animal Rescue in Utah. We send money every month to help take care of her until she gets her forever home. Us kids are all donating part of our chore wages to her."

"That would have to be a big forever home," Esther said.

"And your parents are kicking in, too," reminded her father.

"Big Dog Rescue sends us pictures of her being cute. We can

watch her on their web cam." Sunny twirled.

"You girls did a good thing," said Vee's stepdad, raising his red plastic cup in salute. Immediately the other parents did the same. "To the S.A.V.E. Squad!"

The girls blushed and joined in the applause, laughing and applauding each other with exaggerated bows. Wink, Baba, and Fred aroo-aroo'd!

Aneta—full of chips, guacamole, sour cream, and love—sighed. Yes. They were the S.A.V.E. Squad. It is what they did. It was who they were. Just like she was a Jasper. Aneta Jasper.

Mom's Peanut-Butter Cookie Recipe

1 cup peanut butter
1 cup sugar
1 egg
1 teaspoon vanilla

Set oven at 350 degrees. Mix all ingredients. Shape dough into balls and place on cookie sheet. Bake for 8 minutes.

Kathleen's note: Yes! Those are the ONLY ingredients. My student Emily brought these to class one time, and I fell deep into cookie love. She got the recipe from her grandmother. She says if you are feeling super special, put an unwrapped Hershey kiss on top right after they come out of the oven. P.S. Emily likes to write. Do you?

Lauraine Snelling is an award-winning author with more than sixty-five published titles, including two horse series for kids. With more than two million books in print, Lauraine still finds time to create great stories as she travels around the country to meet readers with her husband and rescued basset, Sir Winston.

Kathleen Damp Wright teaches writing to Christian home-schoolers and can't wait to buy a student's first novel! When she's not dreaming up adventures for her characters, she's riding bikes with her husband, playing pickle ball, and trying to convince her rescued border collie that Mom knows best.